I0603744

JOGGING IS BAD FOR YOUR HEALTH

A Nosy Neighbor Mystery, Book 5

Cynthia Hickey

DEDICATION

To God. Thank you..

ACKNOWLEDGMENTS

To my husband, Tom, who gives up time with me on many weekends so I can finish the latest book. To my editor, Jan, who helps me make the book the best it can be, and to my readers who anxiously await the next cozy mystery. Thank you..

1

I'd managed to kill off another three people. On paper, of course.

I, Stormi Nelson, best-selling author of romantic mysteries, typed The End on my latest manuscript and sent it via email to my agent. That also felt so good. I was especially pleased with the fact that this time, I'd used my imagination to write the book, rather than copy the most recent murder I found myself mixed up in.

Sadie, my beloved Irish Wolfhound, lay her massive head in my lap and looked up at me with soulful eyes. She whined deep in her throat, letting me know we were late for our walk.

"How about a jog?" My mother had taken up the health craze. It wouldn't hurt me to get rid of a little jiggle. Besides, it was my turn on the neighborhood watch, which it normally was, since people were reluctant to join anything I started.

I closed my laptop and slipped my feet into sneakers. "I'm taking Sadie for a walk, er, jog," I called out to anyone listening.

Once upon a time, I'd enjoyed my life as a solitary, introverted writer. That was before my agent sent me out into the world to mingle, and my mother, sister, niece and nephew showed up on my doorstep. How had I managed all alone? Life was more interesting with others around and provided plenty of fodder for my stories. Not to mention my first night "out" introduced me to my love, Matthew Steele, handsomest detective in the Ozarks.

Sadie and I stepped into a warm late September evening and walk/jogged past Matt's house. I knew he was on a case and not home, but I took the chance anyway. Mary Ann, Matt's sister, and my best friend and literary assistant, sat on the front porch with her squeeze, rookie cop, Michael Barker. We exchanged waves and

I continued, my breathing already sounding like I smoked two packs of cigarettes a day for years. I'd never smoked a single one.

I stopped at the corner and bent over to catch my breath. Sadie sat next to me, pink tongue lolling.

"Miss Stormi okay?"

I glanced up at Rusty Henley, neighborhood peeping Tom, simpleton, and resident sweetheart. "I'm … fine."

"Exercise must be started slowly." He shook his head as if I were the slow one and moseyed away, disappearing in the shadow of a large magnolia tree.

He was right. I should walk. Jogging could come later, when I improved my lung function. I might be slim, but writing was a sedentary occupation.

I turned around in a cul de sac, surprised to see a young, very pretty girl sitting on the curb. I guessed her to be fifteen, maybe sixteen-years-old. She twirled a thin stick in a water puddle next to her foot.

"Hello." I smiled.

She jerked, obviously so lost in her

own world she hadn't heard me approach. Eyes wide, she jumped to her feet and raced down the sidewalk in the opposite direction. A light-colored sedan stopped next to her and she climbed in.

Strange. Some people tended to leave a room when I walked in to avoid my endless questions, but few ran away without knowing me. I shrugged and continued.

"Hi, Stormi!" Lucy Snyder, a single mother of four rowdy boys, watered a small garden of flowers. I'd met her while previously researching a murder and found I liked her a lot. I'd put out a few feelers in town and got her a job at the supermarket as a cashier. Because of that, she was able to rent a cute little bungalow in the same community I resided in.

"Hey." I stopped and let Sadie drink from the hose.

"Have you met our new neighbors yet?" She motioned her head to the large house next door. "They keep to themselves, but I've heard it's a foster family. Lots of kids in varying teen ages come and go. Adults, too, come to think of it. I've yet to meet the parents."

"No, the Salazars might have." They were my next door neighbors, little people, and the only other community residents interested in patrolling the neighborhood. I made a mental note to ask them. "Your house is quiet."

"The boys are with my mother." She grinned. "I'm relishing the peace and quiet. They'll be home tomorrow." She shuddered. "I love them with all my heart, but gee whiz! They wear me out. Not to mention the evil looks Mrs. Olson is always giving me."

"She's just warning you away from her husband." Mrs. Olson seemed to think every woman in Oak Meadows Estates had the hots for her portly, balding husband.

"Gross."

"I'll catch you later, Lucy. I don't want my body to forget why I'm torturing it." I tugged Sadie's leash and resumed what was not quite a jog, but rather a fast walk. As I passed the Olson house, I waved. "Good evening, Mr. Olson."

Mrs. Olson glared and turned the hose

in my direction, just barely missing my shoes. I laughed and continued. I shouldn't tease her so, but really, the woman needed to lighten up.

Mrs. Rogers, a former nemesis who tried to have me tarred and feathered and run out of the housing development, gave me a nod. While we might not be bosom buddies, narrowly escaping death together, have formed a bond, of sorts, between us. As long as she was no longer passing around a petition to get rid of me, I'd take what little civility I could get.

"Boo!"

"Rusty!" I put a hand on my chest. "What in the world?"

He laughed and ducked back into the bushes.

I glanced at my dog. "You're supposed to warn me of things like that."

She wagged her tail.

Heart still threatening to beat out of my chest, I continued my walk and fought the urge to leave the gated community and visit my friend Norma at her coffee bar. A former prostitute, Norma had risen above her past to become an influential business owner and a close friend. Willpower being as weak as it was, I headed out the gate and down Main Street.

I looped Sadie's leash around a vintage-style lamp post and headed into Delicious Aroma. Sure enough, my friend sat at a corner table rather than in her office.

"Hey." I sat down across from her and waved to her son, Tyler, to bring me my usual. The largest frozen, blended Mocha they had.

"What brings you out at eight o'clock?" Norma asked, closing her laptop.

"Jogging."

Her laughter was totally uncalled for.

"O-o-o-kay." She snorted and crossed her arms. "Now, tell me the truth."

"That is the truth. I was out jogging," I held up a finger to ward off another bout of loud laughter, "and realized how hard it was and continued walking. It's my job as president of the neighborhood watch."

"Of course it is. You wouldn't be trying to dig up another mystery, would you?"

"It wouldn't hurt if I came across one." I did enjoy sticking my nose where it didn't belong. "Now that I have my private investigator's license…"

"You got it!"

"Came in the mail today." I grinned. "I can now snoop legally."

"As if you needed an excuse."

Tyler brought me my drink, waving off payment as usual.

I took a sip, closing my eyes with pleasure. "Heard any good gossip lately?"

"Not a thing. It's very quiet around Oak Meadows. Has been since the real estate fiasco. That was four months ago."

I was glad we'd managed to stop that whole taking over picturesque downtown so a few people could make a few bucks. It had taken a while for people to stop asking Mom for information regarding the bookstore owner being found dead in a vat of baking chocolate in her bakery, but it hadn't hurt her business any.

"I should probably start heading back." Already I could feel unused muscles tightening in protest at unaccustomed exercise.

"Thanks for stopping by." Norma opened her laptop.

I retrieved my dog and spotted the skittish teenage girl from before getting out of yet another car. She flashed a grin at someone inside before turning as looking as forlorn as a boy who had lost his dog.

She kicked at a rock on the sidewalk, thrusting her hands into shorts barely long enough to be called decent. It wasn't until I took a good look at her face that I noticed the ruby lips and smoky eyes of skillfully applied makeup.

As was normal for me, curiosity reared its head and I decided to follow her.

She ducked between the bakery and the bookstore, now with new owners. I hurried across the street after her.

She turned right at the alley, back toward Oak Meadows Estates, but stopped behind the drugstore. My nephew, Dakota, stepped from the shadows and pulled her into his arms.

Very interesting. He hadn't said anything about having a girlfriend. I pressed against the building, keeping a hand on Sadie's muzzle to keep her quiet.

"I thought you were never going to show," Dakota said.

"I had a hard time getting away," the girl replied. "I only just now snuck out."

"Your foster parents shouldn't keep such a tight rein on you."

The girl was lying. I'd seen her leave her house an hour ago. I wasn't naïve enough to believe teenagers didn't lie, they did, but why would she lie to Dakota?

I averted my face when they started an embarrassingly heavy make-out session. After what seemed like an eternity, they kissed one last time and parted. The girl ducked back between the buildings and Dakota continued in the alley. This time I actually jogged as I caught up with him.

"Hey."

He glanced over his shoulder and scowled. "Are you spying on me?"

"Nope." I held up my coffee. "Jogging and drinking. Who is your friend?"

"Heather Miller. She's new to the

neighborhood." His eyes narrowed, glittering under the street lamp as we stepped onto the sidewalk. "You were watching me."

"Completely by accident." I wrapped my lips around my straw so I wouldn't say more than I should and get myself into trouble.

"We need to help her," he said, his young face hardening. "Her foster parents are horrible. They hardly let her out of the house, and I've seen bruises on her arms and thighs more than once."

"Have you told anyone?"

"I'm telling you." He stopped and faced me. "As your investigating assistant, I'd like this to be our first case."

No one actually said he was my assistant, but he wouldn't hear otherwise. "We can look into it if you think she's being abused. What about the other kids? Have you spoken to them?"

"I've only seen them. There's two other girls. One black and one Mexican. Heather said her foster parents only take in girls. She won't talk much about her home life. If I mention the bruises, she changes the subject."

It definitely sounded like abuse to me. "I'll talk to Matt and see what he has to say."

"We can't get the police involved!" Dakota shook his head. "And you call yourself an investigator. Just ask some questions. Make friends with her mother. Do your job."

"My job is writing books. My PI license is to give me leeway when investigating." I held up a finger as he opened his mouth to protest. "But … I will look into this. My way. And you will remember your manners when speaking to me." I gave him a stern look and strolled away. Yes, strolled. Jogging hadn't done anything that night other than cause me more work. Besides, I didn't want to risk spilling my drink.

I wasn't making light of his friend's plight. To the contrary. Abuse of any living creature did not sit well with me. I'd be knocking on my new neighbor's door come morning.

2

True to my word, the next morning I stood in front of Dakota's friend's house with a baked spaghetti casserole in my hand. To my family's delight, I tended to cook for relaxation and had a full freezer. The spaghetti was the largest casserole I currently had on hand. Balancing the aluminum baking pan in the crook of one arm, I pressed the doorbell.

A tall, very pretty black girl wearing a tee shirt that barely covered parts best left hidden opened the door. My mouth opened and closed like a beached fish. I finally managed to get out, "You look just like this woman…"

"Ivy?" She raised one eyebrow. "Yeah, she's my mother. You must be the person who put her in jail." If she had any trace of friendliness on her face, it fled like chaff on the wind.

"She killed someone."

She shrugged. "And I'm in hell. We all have our problems. What do you want?"

"May I speak with your, uh, foster mom?" I was out of my element for sure.

"Yeah, wait here." She closed the door before I could get a peek of the inside of the house.

The pan in my hands got very heavy before the door opened again. A woman close to six feet tall, dark hair pulled tightly away from her face, and sensible shoes on her feet, glared at me. "Yes?"

"I'm Stormi Nelson, one of your neighbors, and I've brought you a casserole as a welcoming gift." I pasted on my best smile and held out the dish.

She grinned, something between a grimace and a shark getting ready to take a bite out of its prey, and took the offering. "Why, thank you very much. I'm Carol Forbes. You met Melody."

"I heard you're a foster home?" I tried to peer around her. "How wonderful. The world needs more people like you."

"It's a tough job for sure." She moved an inch to the side, effectively blocking any glimpse of the inside I might have gotten. "We're very busy with getting settled. Thank you for stopping by." She closed the door, leaving me on the porch like a bag of garbage.

I glanced at the lawn, badly in need of mowing, and declared right then and there, I'd pay Rusty to do it. That man managed to find out information no one else could. And there was definitely something suspicious about Carol Forbes. I felt it in my gut.

The For Rent sign still stood in the yard, proudly displaying the name of our local realtor, Jane Weston. It wouldn't hurt to pay her a visit and ask a bit more about my new neighbors. On behalf of the Neighborhood Watch, of course.

I hotfooted it back home, grabbed my purse from the foyer table, then headed back out and slid behind the wheel of my new silver Mercedes. I loved new cars. The look and smell of them. And, yes, I admit, the prestige. I worked hard to get where I was, and didn't mind pampering myself a bit. It started with the newly-renovated Victorian I lived in, then spread to the car. Who knew what was next? Maybe a cruise. If my books kept selling the way they did, and Mom's bakery did well, I could pretty much do whatever God placed upon my heart to do.

I stopped by Mary Ann's house to pick her up. "We've another mystery to solve," I said, the moment she got in.

"Who died?" Her blue eyes widened.

"No one, but the new neighbors don't sit right with me. Dakota asked us to take this on as our first official case as private investigators."

"You're making me your partner?" She gripped my arm. "I'm a PI *and* a literary assistant?" Her voice rose several octaves. "Does life get any better than this?"

I laughed and freed myself so I could drive. "Dakota is an unofficial partner. His idea, not mine, since he's underage. Since your job often involves gumshoeing around with me, I thought it only right to make it official."

She clapped her hands. "Matt is going to turn all sorts of red. He hates when I go on sleuthing trips with you."

He wasn't too crazy about me going either, but short of arresting me, there wasn't much the poor man could do. "Let's get our coffee and pay a visit to Jane W." I filled her in on my morning during the short time to Main Street.

"Thank God, there isn't a dead body."

Yet. Give it time. I had the unfortunate gift of stumbling across them, to the dismay of my family.

After purchasing our coffee, we strolled down the sidewalk toward Westin Realty. I stopped and gazed at the houses for sale in the window, dreaming of the time when I had my home to myself. What if Matt and I got married? Would we have to share with my family? I'd already converted the basement into an apartment for Mom, and the attic for my sister. Maybe I would be the one who had to move.

"Come on." Mary Ann bumped me with her shoulder. "You love no longer being alone. Stop daydreaming."

True. I pushed open the door and was immediately assaulted by a sweet air freshener plugged into the wall next to the door. My eyes stung and my nose burned. I practically ran to Jane's desk in order to get away from it as quickly as possible.

"Too strong?" She asked.

"A bit." I sat in one of the chairs across from her, leaving the other for Mary Ann, who was tossing the air freshener in the trash. I wished I'd thought of that.

"Use something more subtle," she said sitting down. "You don't want to cause a prospective client to have an asthma attack."

Jane's eyes narrowed. "Fine. What do you want? I doubt either of you are here to purchase a new home."

"You are correct." I settled into the comfortable padded chair. "I'd like to ask some questions about a new neighbor. Carol Forbes."

Jane frowned. "Why?"

"I've had a complaint that she might be abusing her foster children."

"Ridiculous. The woman came with

impeccable references. I don't do business with scum, Stormi."

I almost brought up the realty scam to purchase all the shops on Main Street. She'd been quite the avid supporter of the idea. But, I wisely kept my mouth shut. Alienating someone with the influence Jane had wasn't a good thing to do.

"If you're sure," I said, pretending to study my nails. I desperately needed a manicure. Typing was hard on a girl's nails. "I wouldn't want someone to pull the wool over your eyes, and I have it on good authority—"

"Whose authority?" She slammed her palms on the desktop.

"A friend of one of the foster children."

"A child?" Her thinly tweezed eyebrows rose almost to the hairline of her bleached blond hair. "You're wasting my time on the word of a child?"

"Can you give me the name of the property owner?"

"Definitely not. It's an investment firm that can't be bothered with such things." She turned to her computer. "And neither can I." She waved her hand in a shooing motion.

"Okay." I stood, shaking my head at Mary Ann's confused expression and led the way out of the office.

"You didn't argue. You always argue." Mary Ann crossed her arms.

"Let's sit on the bench across the street. Just watch." We hurried over and sat, partially obscured by a flowering potted plant.

Less than five minutes later, Jane locked her realty office door and climbed behind the wheel of her Audi. Without a glance in our direction, she sped toward Oak Meadows Estates.

"See?" I grinned. "She can't stand the fact there might be something going on that she isn't aware of. She'll do the snooping for us."

"Will she share the information?"

"I'll argue it out of her if she doesn't."

"What will you do if she is abusing the kids?"

"Turn her into CPS." Nothing made me more angry than abuse…of anything.

Children, women, animals…it didn't matter.

"What now?" Mary Ann wrapped her lips around the straw of her watered down drink. "You finished your latest book. Unless you have a reason to snoop some more, we have a free day."

I sat in shock. When was the last time I had a day with nothing planned? I honestly couldn't remember. A free day and my boyfriend was undercover somewhere. I sighed. Just my luck. "Let's go see what Mom has baking."

We stepped into Mom's shop. Dakota sat at the back work table, stuffing his teenage face with a cupcake.

"Why aren't you in school?" I grabbed one of the chocolate on chocolate cupcakes from in front of him.

"Leave him alone," Mom said. "He's worried about his friend."

"He told you?"

"You certainly didn't."

"I only found out last night. I haven't seen you."

"You could have left a note."

I opened my mouth, had nothing to

say in response, and filled my mouth with cake instead. I glared at my nephew. If he involved my mother in our private investigation business, there'd be no peace in town. She'd think she had a legitimate reason to investigate everyone.

"Seriously, Stormi," Mom said. "Why you don't want me involved in your life is beyond me. I think I've proven myself to be quite the detective. Remember when we were kidnapped? Who was it that snuck away and went for help?"

"You." I sighed. "Fine. Do you have information for me?"

"Not yet." She frowned. "I've only just heard of the alleged abuse. Since I'm the president of the Hickory Hellos, I'll take a cake over tonight and befriend the fiend."

If anything could soften Carol Forbes, it was one of Mom's creations. The devil himself would start singing praises after one bite. Her talent could only be a gift from God Himself.

"I don't want you to go alone. You can't take Dakota and I can't go. I've already made my acquaintance."

"I'll go," Greta said, stepping out of the supply room. "I've just delegated myself second-in-command of the Hickory Hellos. Being a former police officer, I should be able to determine whether the woman is hiding something."

I told them how one of the girls was Ivy's daughter. "If looks could kill, you'd be planning my funeral."

"Well, you're probably the reason she's in foster care," Mom pointed out. "Why shouldn't she be mad?"

I hadn't known Ivy had a daughter. Not that it would have mattered. As a murderous gang leader's girlfriend, and having had a hand in the death of a prostitute, she needed to be put away, mother or not. I refused to feel guilty about Melody. Except, I did.

Now, I needed to find a way to make her life easier. If exposing abuse was the way to do it, then I'd do everything in my power to get to the bottom of my nephew's allegations. One way or the other, I'd do my best to make it up to Ivy's daughter.

3

"I'm off to deliver a cake." Mom held a delicious looking chocolate creation on her second best cake plate. "If I'm not back in thirty minutes, call the cavalry."

"I am the cavalry," Greta said, patting her pocket that had a suspicious gun-shaped bulge.

I wasn't law enforcement, but I was pretty sure she shouldn't be carrying. But, as an ex-cop, she probably had a license. Still, these two women weren't the type you wanted showing up on your doorstep with a gun.

I grabbed Sadie's leash. "I'll follow and stay discreetly in the bushes."

"That isn't necessary." Mom gave me one of her 'looks'. "Greta and I will be perfectly fine."

"I have to walk the dog. I might as well go in the same direction as you."

"Just don't interfere before I can win this woman over." She marched out the door, followed by Greta, leaving me and Sadie to bring up the rear. Sometimes Mom made me feel just like a child again.

I stayed a respectful fifty paces behind them, when in actuality, I wanted to be next to them. When they strolled up the drive to Carol's, I ducked behind a row of evergreen bushes and commanded Sadie to hush. Like a good girl, she plopped on the ground next to me.

Ugh. I wouldn't be able to hear a word from that distance. I doubted whether Carol knew Mom was my mother. Couldn't I nonchalantly stroll down the sidewalk, pausing to tie my shoe at the appropriate time? I didn't see why not.

I coaxed my big lazy dog from her resting place and walked as slow as was possible and still move forward. I'd just reached the end of Carol's driveway when she opened the door. I bent over to tie my shoe. Darn. No laces. They were slip-ons. Maybe that wasn't visible from the house.

Mom stopped frowning at me and

grinned. "We're the Hickory Hellos. You know, since we live on Hickory. We'd like to welcome you to the neighborhood with this cake freshly baked from my bakery, Heavenly Bakes."

"This is the friendliest neighborhood I've ever moved to." Carol took the cake, not sounding at all pleased about the friendliness. In fact, she acted more like it was a bother.

"Do you need help with your shoe?"

I glanced up to see Rusty peering down at me. "No, thanks. Just getting a pebble out." I stood. "How would you like another job mowing this yard?"

"For the same ten dollars you pay me?"

"Of course." I actually made sure eighty dollars got deposited into his account every month, but in Rusty's mind the number ten was larger than eight, even with the y tacked on the end. I couldn't ask him to openly snoop, he'd do that anyway, and voicing the fact would only have him spill the beans if Carol asked. "Wonderful. I'll let the woman know you'll mow in the morning."

"Not too early," he said. "I don't wake up until six."

"I'm sure she would prefer more like eight." I patted his shoulder and moseyed up the drive, pretending like I didn't know Mom or Greta.

Carol was clearly not happy to see me. I couldn't help but wonder what someone had said about me. Still, I smiled. "Good evening. Don't be alarmed in the morning when a young man mows your lawn. It's a gift for being a new neighbor."

She sighed and shook her head. "We don't take charity. I'll pay for it myself. How much?"

"Just hand him ten dollars and he'll be over the moon."

She nodded. "Thank you for visiting. We've had a long day and it's time for bed."

I glanced at my watch. Eight p.m.

A car stopped in front of the house and a curvy girl with thick hair hanging to her waist slid out, tugging a short red dress down to a respectable length. She giggled and closed the door. Her smile immediately faded once the car pulled away. With her head down, face hidden behind her curtain of hair, she made her way up the drive.

"Rosie, greet our new neighbors." Carol's eyes hardened.

The girl, clearly startled, jerked. "Nice to meet you," she said in a thick accent. She scuttled past us and into the house.

Greta's gaze followed the girl into the house, then narrowed when she turned back to Carol. "Teenagers are hard. You have your work cut out for you with three beautiful girls."

"They aren't too bad. Goodnight. Thank you for the cake," she turned to me, "and the lawn." She closed the door.

I didn't speak to Mom or Greta until we were out of sight of the house. "You suspect something, Greta. Out with it."

"Two things." She held up a finger. "One … what mother doesn't seem upset when their daughter gets out of a car half-dressed? Two … that young lady's demeanor changed as soon as the car left. It was like a curtain fell over her face."

"Carol didn't seem happy when Rosie got home," I said.

"Not happy because she looked like she did, or because we were there to see her?" Greta crossed her arms. "I might be seeing something that isn't there, but that girl, Rosie, was scared. Whether of Carol or whoever was in the car, I don't know. Point is … my gut tells me something is going on at that house."

Our guts were in agreement. "Dakota is friends with one of them. He thinks his friend is being abused."

"That's a good explanation. But, before we get CPS involved and disrupt these girls' lives further, we need to do a big more investigating."

Again, in agreement.

"Why not let CPS do the nosing around?" Mom asked.

I looked at her as if she'd grown another eye. "Really? I thought you enjoyed this type of thing."

"I do, but I don't want to alienate a neighbor."

I rolled my eyes. "The important thing here is the girls. I don't think we need to involve CPS yet. They tend to yank the kids and investigate later. Foster kids of this age have already been bounced around enough." I prayed I wouldn't come to regret my decision. Keeping a close eye on Carol's house and its occupants became my top priority, and something I would discuss with Matt when he called.

"Smart move involving Rusty." Greta grinned. "That boy sniffs out trouble better than a hound."

"The hard part is getting the information out of him." I climbed the porch steps and let Sadie into the house before settling on the porch swing. The night carried a definite chill, but sitting and softly rocking always helped clear my head.

I set the swing into motion with my toe and rested my head against the back so I could stare at the stars. It wasn't quite as pleasurable as sitting with Matt. Nor as warm. I wrapped my arms around my middle and ran back over the events of the last two days.

One: Dakota thinks his friend is being

physically abused, thus setting me off on another mystery adventure. Two: Three young girls, all pretty, live with Carol Forbes. All three wear the minimal amount of clothing and seem scared of their own shadows. Three: Greta feels the same as I do … something is fishy at the foster home. Four: I had no idea what to do next.

I closed my eyes and listened to the night around me. A car driving slowly down the street. A dog barking a couple of streets over. The sound of laughter. Wait. That's Dakota. I stilled the swing and peered through the trellis that, in the spring, was covered with climbing roses.

"Just take the money," he said. "I don't want you to get in trouble when you get home."

"I didn't earn it."

"They don't know that." Dakota wrapped her fingers around some cash. "Please. It's all I can do at this point."

She kissed his cheek. "Keeping my secret is enough." She turned and, like a vapor, disappeared around the corner of the house.

My snoop radar was tingling. But, I knew without asking that my nephew would tell me nothing. He was the king of keeping secrets.

My cell phone rang.

Dakota whirled to face the porch. "Aunt Stormi! Were you listening again?"

"Just resting." I fished the phone from my pocket.

"Don't repeat a word of what you might have heard." He banged into the house.

I pressed the on button and shrugged. "Hello?"

"Hey, gorgeous!"

"Matt." Immediately my world fell into place. "This isn't your usual number."

"No, and I only have a few seconds to talk. I love you."

"I love you, too." I wanted to run the foster home questions past him, but also didn't want to waste a single second on anything but listening to his voice. "Are you staying safe?" I knew he couldn't tell me much, but that little bit would settle my fears.

"Pretty much."

That wasn't exactly what I wanted to hear. "I miss you."

"Ditto. But, we're wrapping things up. It appears things might have moved a bit closer to home."

"That's good, I guess." I set the swing back into motion, not entirely sure we wanted whatever crime he was trying to stop from moving closer.

"How are things on your end?"

"There is something that I need to discuss with—"

"Gotta go, babe." Click.

I sighed and slipped my phone back into my pocket. Why couldn't he still be an ordinary street cop like when we first met? Every day I had to remind myself that God loved him more than I did and would watch out for my hunky hero. Still, worry teased at the fringes of my mind on a daily basis.

Cherokee strolled up the sidewalk, swinging her purse, wearing a skirt that cupped her bottom like saran wrap. Maybe that's how all the young girls dressed and nothing was out of the ordinary with Carol's girls. "Hey," I said, as she approached the porch.

"Hey." Her smile was a bright light in the night.

"You seem happy. Date?"

"The best. I met the sweetest boy the other day at work."

"What's his name?"

"Rory." She leaned against the porch railing, looking younger than her just-turned-eighteen age. She showed her Indian heritage and hardly anything from her blond mother. My niece was an exotic beauty. I was surprised she didn't have more boys knocking on the door.

"When do we get to meet him?"

"It's too soon." She flashed a grin and reached for the door handle. "You'll meet him when it's time." She sashayed into the house.

Which sounded like a very good idea. Tiredness coated my shoulders and the cold was starting to seep to my bones. My bed called my name loud and clear.

I stood and stretched.

A cry from the street startled me. I peered through the dark.

Melody stood hunched over on the

opposite sidewalk, the streetlight showcasing her misery. Carol, in a dark-colored van, was stopped next to her.

"Get in right now!" Carol pounded the dashboard.

"I want out. Please." Melody shook her head.

"You know the consequences, Melody. Get in the van."

Melody glanced up, her gaze clashing with mine. Even though I ducked out of sight, I didn't miss her silent cry for help.

4

After tossing and turning for hours, I'd finally fallen asleep when I dreamed of being kissed and of Matt spooning me while I slept. I smiled and rolled over, then realized I wasn't dreaming.

I shrieked and shoved against him. "If Mom sees you, she'll have a fit!"

Laughing, he slid from the bed. "Get up. I've missed you." He yanked the blankets away. His gaze roamed over the shorts and tank top I slept in. "Cute. Come on. I cooked breakfast."

My hero. I leaped from the bed and followed him to the kitchen.

A stack of pancakes sat in the middle of the table. Next to it was a plate of bacon, a bowl of powdered sugar, and a stick of softened butter.

"You're the best!" I threw my arms around his neck and pressed my lips to his, murmuring how much I loved him.

He wrapped his arms around my waist and lifted me off my feet. When our kiss deepened to the point of danger, he set me on the floor and pulled out a chair. "I don't have a lot of time."

"Why?"

"My case has moved here. I'm still working." He wrapped a pancake around three slices of bacon, dribbled syrup over the lot, and took a bite. "If my supervisor finds out I'm here, he'll have my head."

"But everyone in Oak Meadows knows who you are." I slathered butter on my pancakes. "It will be hard to blend in."

"These people don't know me, and I have a disguise. If you recognize me, act like you don't." He kissed me again, tasting of bacon and maple syrup. "I'll try to sneak over tonight. Love you."

"I'll be up. I have something I need your help with. Something important. A child might be in danger."

He got serious, then gave me a curt nod, knowing without me saying a word that I had another mystery to solve. One he probably wouldn't be happy about. What had I done to deserve such a patient man? Not only did he have to deal with me getting into dangerous situations, but my entire family. Sometimes, we went so far as to accidentally impede an investigation. We were quite well known among the local law enforcement.

I finished breakfast, wrapped up the extra pancakes for the others to eat later, then headed to my office to jot some notes. A face appeared at the window. I screamed, then relaxed as I recognized Rusty. I held up a finger to signify he stay there, then rushed outside and around the house.

"Stop doing that. You scared me." Thank goodness I was fully clothed.

"I'm going to mow now."

"Okay."

"Other house."

I nodded, wondering where he was headed with his comments. It didn't do any good to second-guess or rush him.

"She doesn't have a mower."

"Oh, right. You may use mine."

While I was used to his meandering ways of getting to the point, others weren't as accommodating. Someday, I hoped to find a way to communicate to him that it was best to get to the point. "Come back here when you've finished. And, don't forget my tools."

I wanted to get any news he dug up out of him right away. Rusty headed for my tool shed, and I went to the front of the house. Mary Ann pulled into the driveway.

"Hey. Matt's home."

"I saw him this morning."

"But we have to act like we don't know him. He's staying in one of those rent by the week places on the highway."

I shuddered, imagining him sharing a room with hundreds of roaches and eating fast food three times a day. My poor Matt. "Any idea what his case is about?"

"Nope. That man is as tight-lipped as a … well, I can't think of anything that isn't a cliché. Are we going for coffee?"

"Let me get dressed." I raced into the house, leaving her to follow and took the stairs two at a time to my room. Nothing got me moving as fast as the promise of one of Norma's delicious coffees. That, and I wanted to ask her to keep her ears open as to the goings on at the home of Carol Forbes. With Tyler having graduated high school this past spring, he might still have an "in" with the young crowd. At least she hoped so.

Ten minutes later, my legs encased in skinny jeans, my feet in ballet flats, and me wearing a red, long-sleeve tee shirt, I tied my hair into a messy bun and hurried back downstairs to where Mary Ann stood at the kitchen window.

"Rusty sure is digging through your shed."

"He's borrowing some tools to use on the foster home yard. Ready?"

She nodded. "He takes out one thing, puts it back, then takes out another. He really is the strangest thing."

"But harmless. He's keeping busy. He'll make it to his job soon enough." I rubbed my hands together. "Now, let's go get that coffee."

"Oh, I see. He put back a rusty rake and took a fairly new one. He's a picky gardener."

I guess I needed to buy some new tools for him to use. Or, better yet, buy him his own. After all, other than the inheritance left by his mother, he lived off what he made doing lawns.

"Now, he has a box."

I peered over her shoulder. "That's not mine." I'd never seen the small cardboard box before. From between the flaps hung what looked like long black tresses. I opened the kitchen door. "What's that, Rusty?"

"Nothing." He hunched over the box and lumbered out of sight.

"I'll figure out what he's up to later." I locked the door, set the alarm, and followed Mary Ann to her car. Things like coffee and gossip took priority.

I waved at Tyler and made a beeline for Norma's table. I'd long ago quit trying to figure out why she preferred doing her work in the business of the coffee shop over her quiet office. When I wrote, I didn't need, or want, any distractions.

"Hey."

"Hey," she answered, closing her

laptop. "What questions can I answer today?"

"You know me so well." I sat down. "I'm actually asking your permission to have Tyler do a bit of snooping."

"He's eighteen. He doesn't need my permission. Is it dangerous?"

"I'm not sure." I told her of my feelings toward Carol Forbes and her charges.

"This can't be good. Considering my former profession and what I learned there, I'm warning you to be careful." She tapped her pencil against a pad of paper. "Want me to ask some of the girls if they know anything?"

"Sure."

"If it's what I think it might be, the prostitutes won't be too happy that Forbes moved to town."

"What do you think it is? Something other than abuse?" My blood chilled.

"Oh, it's definitely abuse. I don't want to say more until I know more. Give me a few minutes to make a couple of calls." She pushed away from the table and headed to her office.

Just great. Now she wanted privacy.

Mary Ann brought our drinks over and pulled up a chair. "Where'd she go?"

"To make some calls."

A few minutes later, a very grave Norma returned and stared across the table at us. "Ladies, the girls wouldn't talk. Said they valued their lives too much to say anything other than a young man with lots of money could find out more than we can." She glanced at Tyler. "You can ask my son, but I'm going to pray that he says no."

"Then I won't ask him. Whether he's an adult or not doesn't mean I want to go against your wishes. I'll find out what I need to know another way." Through Rusty or my own sheer nosiness and reckless way of heading straight into trouble. "Do you have a gut feeling?"

She took a deep breath. "Ask your boyfriend what's going on."

"You know he won't tell me." I set my drink down hard enough to splash some through the hole in the lid. "Especially if it's part of his investigation."

It bothered me to learn that the quaint little town of Oak Meadows had the same evil lurking behind its closed doors that the larger cities did. Perhaps prostitution and drugs were more rampant outside our boundaries, but they managed to make their presence known as I had discovered all too well a few months before. As more and more people moved to the Ozarks, crime increased. Soon, if it hadn't already, the very things we encountered elsewhere would rear their ugly heads on our vintage-styled streets.

I wished Norma would tell me, but once she decided not to say anything, not even torture would get the information out of her. I sighed and sipped my drink, trying to decide on our next move. Dakota would be happy to nose around, but I feared he was already involved and if it was as dangerous as Norma acted, I didn't want him in any deeper.

I turned my head and gazed out at Main Street. The bright autumn day had lost a lot of its brilliance. Instead, a cloud covered the sun, casting the town in shadow. Fitting for what seemed to be creeping steadily closer to our fair city.

A car I didn't recognize parked in front of Mom's bakery. Two men in expensive suits climbed out.

I jumped to my feet. "See you. Let me know if you decide to tell me anything." I motioned my head toward the door for Mary Ann to follow and chased after my instincts.

I barged into Mom's shop as the two gentlemen stepped up to the counter. Mom's grin blinded me from the door.

"Welcome to Heavenly Bakes. How may I help you?"

The oldest of the two, a man with silver hair slicked back from his face, leaned just a tad closer to Mom. "We're hosting a party at the end of the week and are hoping we can hire you to cater the dessert table."

Her smile widened. "For how many?"

"Two hundred."

Her eyes widened. "Oh. Well..."

"We'd love to." I stepped forward and offered my hand. "Stormi Nelson, and this is my mother and partner, Anne Nelson. Please, take a look at our catalog and let us know what appeals to you.

His gaze swept from my head to my feet, sending a chill over my spine. "If anything in the catalog looks as delicious as you, then we'll have no problem choosing."

I sincerely hoped we were talking about desserts. The look in his eyes said otherwise. "Is there a theme to your party?"

"Formal. We ask that our servers also dress befitting the occasion." He handed me a business card. "Please be ready to set up at five. Party begins at seven. There is no need for us to look at the catalog. We trust the judgment of professionals." He winked, smiled at Mom, then he and his silent sidekick left the shop.

"That has to be the weirdest order I've ever received." Mom shrugged and opened the catalog. "It'll be easy enough to make mini eclairs and petits. Maybe we can ask Norma to supply coffee to go with the desserts. I think things that can be eaten with fingers are best, don't you?"

I nodded, and glanced out the window. The silver-haired man stood next to his Volvo and stared. When our eyes met, he nodded, then slid into the passenger seat. Again, I felt as if someone had stomped on my grave.

I read the card in my hand. Nicholas Bomberg of Bomberg Enterprises. On the back of the card was written "Where fantasy and life meet". Why did I have a sudden need for a shower?

5

"I need your help." Dakota grabbed my arm later that evening as I strolled around the corner of the house after taking out the garbage.

"A little rough." I yanked free. "Use your words." I saw the roll of his eyes in the light from the kitchen window.

"I think Heather is in some big trouble. She's always out at night, always needs money…" He shook his head. "I help her when I can, but what if she's into drugs and I'm enabling her?" He leaned against the side of the house. "I really like her, Aunt Stormi. Have you found out anything?"

I didn't know much and wasn't sure what I should say about what I did know. "We're looking into the alleged abuse like you asked."

"You think she stays gone all the time because Mrs. Forbes is mean to her?" Hope leaped across his face.

"It's a possibility." I didn't want to go where my mind seemed to be straying. Something about the horrified look on Norma's face after she made a phone call still bothered me. Now Matt was home, in disguise, because his case moved here. Whatever was going on was not good. In fact, my gut told me whatever it was would turn this town upside down.

"I thought so, too, at first, but now…" he shrugged. "I don't know what to think."

"Just keep being her friend."

"I will, but it's hard. She said we have to keep it a secret that she spends time with me."

"Maybe she isn't allowed to date."

His eyes widened. "We aren't dating. Why would I want to be tied down like that?" He shook his head and bounded into the kitchen.

I watched through the window as he grabbed a pint of ice cream from the freezer before heading for the living room. Kids. They bounced back so quickly.

A hand clamped onto my shoulder.

I screamed and whirled.

Rusty grinned, his teeth white through the light of dusk. "I brought your tools back."

"Don't scare me like that." I crossed my arms. "Tell me what was in the box you took out this morning."

"A wig and dirty clothes."

Okay. Not sure I wanted to know why those things were in my shed. "What did you hear or see at the foster house?" I hated to sound demanding, but if I wanted to get information from Rusty, it had to be stated very clearly and concisely or the conversation went in circles until I was ready to pull my hair out.

"Cars come and go. Girls come and go. Girls hand money to lady. Girls cry a lot."

"Did you see the lady hit the girls?"

He shook his head. "When I peek in window, lady close curtains. She looks mean. She scares Rusty."

"She scares me, too." I bit the inside

of my lip. "Can you do more work there tomorrow?"

"I trim bushes tomorrow." He turned and walked away.

I guess the conversation was over. I sighed and headed for the house. The night was cooling off and I still needed to walk Sadie and make our rounds of the neighborhood.

I glanced at my neighbor's house, the Salazars. The windows were still dark. They couldn't return from vacation soon enough to suit me. I needed help with the Neighborhood Watch program. If people didn't see me consistently monitoring the streets, they'd have no inclination to join. I shoved aside the fact that it was almost a year since I'd started the Watch, and we only had four members; Me, Mom, and the Salazars, and Mom rarely fulfilled her obligation. She was either busy concocting new creations for her bakery, or spending time with her banker boyfriend, Robert Smithfield.

I went into the house, grabbed Sadie's leash, and called her away from where she begged for a bite of Dakota's ice cream.

The television was tuned to one of those reality channels about cars driving too fast and crashing. Not my idea of entertainment, but then, I wasn't a teenage boy.

"Come on, girl." I bent over and clicked the leash onto her collar. "We both need a walk more than we need dessert."

"The view looks just fine from where I'm standing."

I jerked upright and turned to see Matt standing in the doorway. "Don't stare at my rear end! It's the biggest part of me."

"Just the way I like it." He gave me a crooked grin that set my stomach to fluttering. "Mind if I walk with you?"

"Don't you need to keep a low profile?"

"I'm not in disguise. It won't hurt for folks to see me with you once in a while. In fact, I want people to know your knight in shining armor is back." He stepped forward and wrapped his arms around me.

I immediately melted into him.

"Now that I'm officially grossed out, I'm going to my room." Dakota turned off the television and took his ice cream with him.

I laughed. "I'd love to take a walk with you." I handed him Sadie's leash and slid my hand into his free one.

Once we were outside, I asked, "Can you tell me about your case?"

"No. Will you tell me about yours?"

I knew he'd say no, but it never hurt to try. I filled him in on everything I'd done over the last couple of days, starting with Dakota's request of help and ending with my conversation with Rusty.

Matt stayed quiet during and after my monologue. I stared at his profile, just making out his features in the light of street lamps as we passed. I wanted to ask him what he was thinking, but experience had taught me he'd only tell me when he felt it safe. No amount of cajoling would get him to utter a word.

His hand tightened on mine. "I want you to step back from this."

"But, Melody asked for my help. I know she did." I stopped and faced him. "Those girls are in trouble, Matt."

He put his hands on my shoulders.

"You have to trust me on this. Your involvement will be dangerous to your entire family, especially Cherokee. Please, stay away."

"What do I tell Dakota? Oh." Nausea rose as my heart plummeted to my knees. "You're talking sex slavery, aren't you?"

"I can't say anything, Stormi. You know that."

I was more determined than ever to help those girls. I'd send my sister and her children to the mountain cabin. They'd be safe there. I was too old to be worried about abduction, right? Tears burned my eyes. It seemed as if every month I had a reason to send my family away for their protection.

What had started out as a hobby to help sell books had turned into something much more. The desire to not only write about my investigating, but to help me, consumed me. I gazed into Matt's eyes, knowing how much my answer was going to disappoint him.

"I have to help."

He rested his forehead against mine. "How could I so desperately love such a stubborn woman? Your heart is one of the things I love most about you, but this isn't a game. These people are dangerous."

"Can't you close down the house?"

"I could, but that wouldn't stop those in charge. I need the top man in order to stop this atrocity." He sighed and pulled me close.

I rested my cheek against his chest, hearing the reassuring thump of his heart. He was a good man, and I understood why he couldn't make a rash move. As much as he worried about me, I worried ten times that much about him. Life was simpler before he made detective.

"I can promise that I won't actively accuse anyone," I said. "I'll help from behind the scenes so you can do your job."

"At least it's something." He gave me a shaky smile that did nothing to reassure me.

While I couldn't stop getting involved in these mysteries that seemed to pop up on a regular basis, I still feared Matt would lose patience with me and call off our relationship. That would kill me. I knew the murder of my father, and the fact his killer was never brought to justice, was at the root of my obsession. It didn't stop me. I still plowed ahead, disregarding the danger. I was a fool.

"Did you just wipe your tears on my shirt?" Matt tilted my face to his.

"Yes. It'll dry before anyone sees."

"Don't cry, sweetheart. I promised to always protect you."

"Who's going to protect you from me?"

He chuckled. "You aren't as dangerous as you think you are."

We resumed our walk, my hand in his, and smiled at the neighbors we passed. When we got close to Carol Forbes's place, I stopped and stepped behind a tree.

"What are you doing?" Matt stood on the sidewalk, head tilted.

"Hiding. Come here."

"If I come in the bushes with you, we'll do more than quietly hide." His voice held a threat of kisses. "I've been sorely deprived since coming home."

Face burning, I grabbed his arm and yanked him down. "Hush, silly. We can't make-out in plain sight." Gracious, they'd forgotten themselves once, falling over themselves on her porch, and Stormi's mother still brought up the embarrassing fact at every opportunity.

"Okay." Matt squatted next to me. "I'll bite. Why are we hiding?"

"I don't want to be seen by Carol Forbes."

"She must be used to your nightly walks by now." He stood. "It's too cold to cower behind the junipers. Come on, scaredy-cat." He held out his hand. "The best way to hide is to act normal. Oh, wait. You are acting normal … for you."

I punched him in the arm and marched down the sidewalk ahead of him so he couldn't see how much I enjoyed his teasing. I missed him so much when he was gone that it was a constant ache.

A white car pulled past us and into Carol's driveway. A woman in dress pants and white blouse got out and opened the back door of the car. A pudgy girl with multiple piercings and one side of her head shaved, shoved past her and marched toward the house. I could hear the woman's sigh from where I stood. Her shoulders slumped as she followed the teen.

They rang the doorbell and waited.

I stepped into the shadow of a magnolia tree and motioned for Matt to be quiet.

"Hello." Carol, smiling wider and looking happier than I'd ever seen her, opened the door wide. "You've brought me another daughter to love."

"Whatever." The girl stormed into the house.

"She's a difficult one," the CPS worker said. "We're having a tough time finding a permanent placement for her."

"Oh, she'll settle in just fine."

Carol's words sent chills down my spine. The newcomer might not fit the mold of the other girls, but I had a feeling that wouldn't stop Carol.

My stomach lurched. Another fly had gotten trapped in evil's web. I turned and buried my face in Matt's chest.

"What can we do?"

"I'm working on it." He wrapped his arms around me. "As fast as I can. If I rush it, we might save these girls, but doom a lot of others."

"So, they're collateral damage?" I peered up at him. How could he be so callous?

"I didn't say that. You have to trust me."

I sighed and stepped back. I'd try. That's all I could do. With one more glance at Carol's house, I turned toward home. The neighborhood was on its own for the rest of the evening. I needed to soothe my worries with hugs from Matt and prayers to God.

"I'm sorry I can't tell you more," Matt said.

"I understand." Truthfully I did, but it still rankled that we couldn't storm that house.

We hadn't gone ten steps before a scream rent the air. We turned as Rusty bolted from the side of the house.

Carol yanked open the front door. "Don't come back. We'll mow our own yard." She slammed the door.

Rusty shrieked when he saw us. "The new girl is bad. She took off her clothes and smiled at me." He raced away.

I didn't know whether to laugh or be stunned. I'd told him countless times not to peek in people's windows. Sooner or later he was bound to see something that would scar his innocent mind forever. Still, I had counted on him digging up information.

"He's going to get arrested one of these days," Matt said.

Expelling air sharply out of my nose, I slipped my hand in Matt's and started again for home.

6

The house alarm woke me at two a.m. The shrill sound cut through my nightmares of dead teens and almost ripped my heart from my chest. I bolted out of bed, grabbed my pink nine-millimeter from the nightstand drawer and thundered downstairs.

"I have a gun!" I slipped on a throw rug and skid to a halt in front of my niece's shocked face.

"When did you get that?" She frowned and punched in the code to disable the alarm.

"A while ago. Why are you just now getting home?" I glanced up the stairs. If Angela found out, we'd have to hear her lecture for hours.

She hid behind her curtain of hair. "I lost track of time." She tugged the neckline of her tee shirt up and the hem of her skirt down. "Don't tell Mom." She brushed past me and headed upstairs.

While my sister and I rarely saw eye-to-eye on anything, I was pretty sure that we would agree that two a.m. was inappropriate for an eighteen year old to come strolling in the door. Still, I wasn't a narc, and Cherokee *was* legally an adult. That didn't mean I wouldn't be keeping a close eye on her. Especially with all that had happened over the last few days.

I peeked out the window, didn't notice anything out of the ordinary, and headed back to bed. Before he went to school, I'd see whether Dakota knew his sister's boyfriend's last name. It wouldn't hurt to have Matt run his name through the system.

Before I could get upstairs, Angela came into the house and reset the alarm. The whole household would be awake soon at this rate.

She gave me a sheepish smile. "Fell asleep watching a movie."

"Sure." Who was I to judge? There were plenty of times I'd like to succumb to temptation, but I held tight to a vow I made in high school, and Matt respected my decision. I've often wondered if that's why the love scenes in my books are so moving, because I've put all the pent up emotions into them.

"Why do you have your gun?" Her eyes widened. "Were you going to shoot me?"

"Only if you were an intruder." I shrugged and headed back to bed. The sun would be up way earlier than I would want.

The next time I opened my eyes, the sun streamed through a crack in the bedroom curtains, promising a warmer than normal day for late September. The clock showed eight a.m. and the doorbell rang with a ferocity to match Sadie's barking.

By the time I got downstairs, no one was there. I glanced down and lifted Mom's cake plate from the doormat. At least they returned it. I would have liked to speak with whichever girl had dropped it off, though. How could I get close enough to them to ask questions without the eagle eyes of Carol seeing me?

Would casual conversation go against the promise I made Matt? It wasn't accusing anyone of anything, or even putting myself in danger. I would only be checking on the welfare of some teens that had been dealt a rough blow by life.

"What's all the racket?" Mom asked as I entered the kitchen.

"Someone brought back your plate." I set it in the sink.

"And this morning?"

"Angela and Cherokee coming home."

She nodded. "My granddaughter has been late a lot lately. I haven't decided whether to tell Angela or not."

"Me, either. She's eighteen, and her mother does the same thing. I doubt she'd listen to us."

"I'm heading to the mall in a bit to find something to wear to this party thing on Friday. Want to go with me? Greta will watch the shop, then she'll go when I get back. Mr. Bomberg called again to remind us that even the hired staff wears formal dress."

"Unless I want to wear something of Angela's, I'd better go with you." I doubted my sister would ever lend me another item of clothing. The last two dresses I borrowed for dates with Matt ended up ruined because of me either being shot at or beat up. It would be best if I ruined a dress of my own this time.

I guessed we decided against church that morning. After changing into my usual clothing of jeans and a tee shirt, I grabbed a yogurt and climbed into the passenger seat of Mom's van. I sent Mary Ann a text, telling her to take the morning off.

"A formal looking pants suit. The dresses for women my age make me look frumpy."

I dug into my meager breakfast. "I'm thinking something slinky and black. Sexy. I'm going to do some snooping and men don't know how to say no to a woman oozing sex appeal." I just hoped I could pull off the charade without falling off whatever heels I bought.

"Great idea! Greta and I can hold down the fort while you mingle. Make sure to iron your hair. You want it to look like liquid fire. Oh, and wear red lipstick. Men can't think around a woman with red lipstick."

"Yes, Mom. Don't forget to stop for coffee."

"You could buy another house with what you spend on frou-frou coffee." She stopped in front of Delicious Aroma. "Bring me back something."

I hurried in, placed our orders with a kid I didn't know, and gazed around the room. No Norma, no Tyler. Oh, well. I didn't have time to talk anyway. If my friend had information for me, she'd call or text.

Five minutes later, drinks in hand, I rejoined my mother and we started the hour drive to Little Rock.

"What's new with the foster girls?"

"A fourth girl joined them last night. I guess she caught Rusty peeking and did a strip-tease. Almost frightened the poor man to death." I laughed. "Can't say I haven't warned him plenty of times. Now, he isn't allowed over there to do any work."

"You'll have to find a new spy." Mom pressed her lips together. "Greta thinks the girls are sex slaves."

I choked on my drink. "I'm starting to think the same thing." I explained Matt's subtle hints and how he's going after whoever is at the top of the organization. "I could be completely wrong about Bomberg, but his business card sounds sleazy enough for him to be involved, don't you think?"

She shrugged. "It could just be something like a *toy* convention."

"Gross. Change of subject." Although, I'd take that over what I feared was really going on.

When we reached the mall, we skipped the large department stores and hit the specialty boutiques. I found several dresses to try, but knew the instant I put on the second dress that there was no need to try another. The black dress fit like a glove, falling off one shoulder, covering the other with a four inch strap, and skimming my hips to fall to the floor with a flirty little kick of a hem. The back plunged to my waist. I felt prettier than I'd ever felt in my life.

I chose a pair of sparkling red heels and dangling red earrings. No necklace, no bracelet, nothing to take away from the power of the dress. I refused to cringe at the price tag, paid for my purchase, and sat on a small white sofa in front of the store to wait for Mom. While I waited, I watched out the window.

Spotting Heather, Melody, and Rosie strolling in and out of people and handing out business cards to men, I handed my dress and shoes to the cashier. "Hold these, please." I dashed out the door and into the atrium.

Once men had a card in hand, they ogled the girls like they were prime sides of beef. It was enough to make my stomach churn.

"Put your eyes back in your head," I ordered one particularly lascivious old fart.

I knew I couldn't interfere, not without breaking my promise to Matt, but that didn't mean I couldn't keep a discreet distance between me and the girls and make sure no one bothered them.

Dakota darted out from the record store, grabbed Heather's arm, and dragged her to the food court. Now, I was safe to make an approach. "Dakota Nelson!"

He stepped in front of Heather. The chivalrous gesture melted my heart but not my resolve.

"How did you get to the mall, and why are you here?"

"I came with you."

"What?"

"I heard you and Grandma talking, knew Heather was coming, and laid quiet in the back of the van."

I scratched my head. "How did you plan on getting home?"

He shrugged. "I would have figured it out when the time came."

I motioned my head toward the hall leading to the restrooms. "You two follow me. We'll have more privacy over here."

Clearly worried about what her friends were thinking, Heather glanced in their direction before following me. "I can't be long. My friends are patient and close-mouthed, but—"

"No need to explain. I'm more

worried about my nephew than you." So not true, but I needed to gain her trust and Dakota was the easiest weapon I had at my disposal. "You can't be sneaking off to meet girls without letting people know where you are. Why is your relationship such a secret anyway?" I glanced at Heather.

"It's complicated," she said, avoiding my eyes. "Dakota is a good friend. Nothing more."

"Not allowed to date?" I did my best to look sympathetic rather than nosy.

"Something like that," she mumbled.

"Stop being nosy." Dakota glared and took Heather's hand. "Come on, before she asks for your blood type."

"You asked for my help. Don't forget that!"

He glanced over his shoulder, holding a finger over his lips.

"What do you need help with?" Heather looked from him to me.

"Nothing. Let's go."

"I think it would be the best thing for you, Dakota, if you were waiting by the fountain in exactly thirty minutes." There.

I'd done my best imitation of a bossy aunt and, hopefully, kept Dakota's reputation intact. I didn't know anything more than I did a few minutes ago, but if my plan worked, Heather might start looking at me and Dakota as people she could trust. And, I'd managed to act outraged in front of the other girls. If there was anything I could do for them, I prayed they'd find a way to come to me.

Melody met my gaze, then turned away. The other girl, Rosie, set her jaw and stared. She wouldn't be easy to win over. I smiled and headed to retrieve my dress.

As I passed a store closed for renovations, I almost ran over Carol as she stepped into the main thoroughfare. "Oh, hello." I glanced around, hoping that Dakota was no longer with Heather.

"Hello." Carol tried looking around me, but I shifted my weight.

If Dakota was still with the girls, he needed time to see what was happening so he could break free. "I don't remember the malls being this crowded when I was young," I said, smiling. "I guess kids have more money now."

"I guess. Excuse me." She pushed me aside.

No matter. I could see the girls and my nephew was nowhere in sight. I breathed a sigh of relief and stepped into the boutique where Mom was purchasing her outfit. I retrieved my gown and shoes before joining Dakota outside the boutique doors.

"That was close," he said, leaning against the wall.

"I wish you'd tell me what is going on."

"The picture is getting clearer. I grabbed this off the floor where some man tossed it." He handed me Bomberg's business card. Only these had a phone number written on the back. "I called it, but the woman on the other end didn't make any sense. She said I was too young to be calling. They only cater to adult men. What does that mean?"

It meant I'd be giving Matt the business card.

7

"Here." I handed the business card to Matt when he came over later that night.

He read the card and scowled. "Where did you get this?"

"Carol's girls were handing them out at the mall." I pulled a quilt over me. The look on Matt's face chilled the living room by twenty degrees. Not that I feared he'd turn that simmering anger on me, not at all, but I still thought it wise to let him process the information quietly.

He pulled out his cell phone.

"What are you doing?" I stiffened.

"Calling the number on the back. It looks like I'll be attending a party on Friday."

Oh. "Me and Mom are, uh, serving at that party." Wait for it. One, two…

"Excuse me?" His brows rose as he

turned to face me on the sofa.

"In our defense, we didn't really know what we were agreeing to. Of course, Mr. Bomberg's request that I wear a formal dress triggered a little warning, but—"

"A little?" He leaned his head back. "Why am I not more surprised?"

I shrugged. "Used to it, I guess." The poor thing. I really did put him through a lot of turmoil.

"Is it worth mentioning that you need a dress that allows you to carry your gun?"

"I don't think the one I purchased does. Oh!" I turned to him. "I can strap it to my inner thigh like they do in the movies."

He sighed. "And walk like a duck? Not very sexy. I'll have to try and keep an eye on you while figuring out what, exactly, is going on at the party."

"I'll stash my gun under the table. You concentrate on what's more important. Saving those girls."

He caressed my cheek with the back of his thumb. "As frustrating as you are, you're the most important thing to me. I'll be keeping an eye on you, too. Wanna go get an ice cream?"

"Sure." I tossed off the quilt. It was never too chilly for a double mint chocolate with my honey.

"We need to go over some ground rules before Friday."

And he ruined the moment. I slung the strap of my purse over my shoulder and followed him to his truck. "You do know what happens every time we go on a date, right?" I said, clicking my seatbelt into place.

"I'm hoping you haven't angered anyone enough this time around for them to shoot at us." He cut me a sideways glance. "You said you weren't going to confront anyone."

"I haven't! Not one single accusation. When I caught Dakota hanging out with Heather, I focused my scolding on him."

"He's befriended one of the girls?" Matt's face darkened. "Does he know what they're into?"

"I think he's beginning to suspect. Heather has asked for help, and—"

"He asked for yours." He leaned his forehead on the steering wheel. "Why do these things happen to your family?"

"We're lucky." I forced a grin.

He groaned and turned the key in the ignition. A few minutes later, we parked in front of the ice cream parlor and chose a table by the window. Why? I had no idea. Sitting in front of a wide expanse of glass always seemed to spell trouble.

I hunched down in the booth and grabbed my menu. The day called for something stronger than chocolate mint. I chose a double hot fudge sundae.

"Relax." Matt smiled over the top of his menu. "I sat in front of the window so you could get over your fear."

"It only takes one bullet to get me over the fear permanently." I peered out the window.

Main Street looked so peaceful, innocent, like another time with its vintage street lights, ornate iron benches, and barrels of flowers. Still, man lived there, and some of those men carried evil in their hearts and wanted to stop nosy people like me from helping those they'd chosen as their victims.

"That's the car that stops by Carol's a lot." I pointed out the light-colored sedan. Of course, the light over the license plate was out so we couldn't read the numbers.

Matt jotted down a description on a napkin and stuck it in his pocket. "That's one more thing I didn't know. You're good at this."

"But, you worry anyway."

"I can't help it. You might have your PI license, but you're my girl."

His words warmed me more than any fire could. No matter what trouble I got into, as long as Matt loved me and God stayed at my side, nothing earthly could harm me. Well, not until it was my time to go, but if I dwelled on that thought for too long, I'd scare myself again.

"Have you written about any of this?"

"No." I frowned. "It didn't even occur to me. I thought of those girls' plight and haven't written a word." I grinned. "Maybe I'm not as much of an opportunist as some reviewers think."

He chuckled. "Don't they say to write what you know? That's all you're doing.

But, I'm glad you're letting this one lie. The girls deserve their privacy."

Out the window, I spotted Dakota skateboarding down the opposite sidewalk in the direction the sedan had gone. I met Matt's gaze and we both bolted from our seats. Matt tossed some money on the table. Ice cream forgotten, we took off after my nephew.

Our feet pounded against the pavement as we raced to keep him in sight. If not for Matt holding my hand and dragging me along, I would have fallen back shortly after getting started. I may take regular walks, but I remembered immediately why I'd given up jogging. It made your heart race and your breath come in gasps.

Dakota stopped at a red light, allowing me a moment to catch my breath. The light turned green all too soon and he took off on four wheels again. What kind of bearings did he have on that board?

"You all right?" Matt glanced at me.

Not having enough breath to speak, I nodded and waved a hand in what I hoped was a gesture for us to continue. I must have gotten it right, because Matt set off at a quick pace again with me tugging my hand free. I leaned against the brick wall of the bank and waved him on. I'd catch up later. Maybe when we met in Heaven. I really was having a heart attack. Maybe.

By the time I could breathe well enough to follow Matt and Dakota, neither one of them was anywhere in sight. All of a sudden, I felt very vulnerable. Whether I'd been sticking my nose into Carol's business or not, asking questions of the neighbors, I still felt as if someone would suspect I was up to something and try to stop me.

I stepped back into the alcove in front of the bank's door and prayed the shadows would hide me. I knew it was futile the moment a squad car pulled up to the curb.

The window rolled down. "Step into the light." The beam of a flashlight blinded me.

"It's me." I stepped out and came face-to-face with my sister's latest flavor of the week, Wayne Jones.

"Why are you skulking around the bank?"

"I'm not skulking." I shaded my eyes. "I'm waiting for Matt."

"Where did he go?" The light blinked off and Wayne got out of the car.

"After Dakota."

He crossed his massive arms. "Are you going to answer in monosyllables or tell me what I need to know?"

"Fine." I filled him in on everything that had been happening, leaving out the fact that Matt was still working undercover. I was sure his former partner knew that, but it wasn't my place to say.

Wayne glanced in the direction I'd pointed. "Get in." Without waiting for me to comply, he slid back into the driver's seat.

Before I had the door closed, he was pulling away from the curb. I studied his hard profile, coming to the conclusion he knew something I didn't, and that something was something to worry about. "What?"

"Nothing."

"Don't be evasive, Wayne! My nephew is out there."

"There's a lot going on right now,

Stormi. Things you don't need to get involved in."

"Tell me something I don't know."

"I can't." He glanced at me. "Just don't trust anyone, no matter how close you think they are."

"You're scaring me."

"Good. Matt will thank me."

We turned the corner and spotted Matt bending over a body in the street. I was out of the car before it came to a complete stop.

"Dakota!"

"It isn't him." Matt stood. "He's hiding in the alley. You might want to go to him."

I spared the poor boy on the street a second glance, then entered the alley, holding out my arms. Dakota ran into them, bending his head to my shoulder. Sobs shook his body. "That's Brian. He's a friend of mine."

I patted his back. "Do you know what happened?"

"No, but I think he was spending time with Rosie, Heather's foster sister."

Ice ran through my veins. If spending

time with one of the girls could result in a young man's demise, would this sweet boy in my arms be next? I wanted to order him not to see Heather again, but I wasn't his mother, and I knew from prior experience that a teenager will be more inclined to do something you order them not to.

I held him at arm's length. "What did you see?"

"Not here." Matt took us both by the arm and ushered us to the squad car. "Wait until we get to the station. Wait in the car. The ambulance is on its way."

"He's alive?" Hope leaped in my chest.

"Yes. He's beaten up pretty bad, but he's breathing." He closed the car door as sirens wailed in the distance.

I reached over and gripped Dakota's hand. "Maybe Brian can tell us what happened."

"Or maybe he'll be too afraid."

8

Wayne must have called my sister, Angela, because she was pacing the front steps of the station when we arrived. No sooner had the squad car door opened, than she had Dakota smashed against her silicone enhanced bosom. Did they still use silicon? I shrugged. It was too late to be contemplating what made up my sister's "girls".

Matt held out a hand to help me from the squad car. Concern clouded his features. "Are you all right?"

"I'm fine. Let's get Dakota's statement and go to the hospital to check on Brian. Dakota is going to be worried." I was, too. There was something about seeing a young man, someone's child, lying in the road unresponsive, that ripped at your heart.

"We'll go as soon as we're able." Matt unlocked the door to the precinct and ushered the rest of us in as Wayne slid from behind the driver's wheel of the police car.

He hurried to Angela's side, slipping an arm around her waist to pull her close.

I shook my head. Who was the wounded one…her or Dakota? I took my nephew's hand and followed Matt to an interrogation room.

"I'll sit with him." Angela pushed past me into the room. "I'm his mother."

"Then act like it and stop seeking attention for yourself." I crossed my arms and joined Wayne in the next room.

He frowned at my presence, but didn't comment as I stepped up to the one-way mirror. I must have earned my right to be there by now. After all, I'd helped the under-staffed police department catch several killers. Often at great danger to my own life.

After fifteen minutes, it was clear Dakota didn't know anything. When Matt had caught up to him, he'd been kneeling beside Brian. He said he'd found him that way.

"What do you know about Bomberg Enterprises?" Matt asked.

"Who?" Dakota's brow furrowed, and he glanced at his mother.

"What do you know about Heather's job?" Matt wrote something on a pad of paper in front of him.

"She doesn't have a job. That's why I'm always giving her money."

"What?" Angela snapped to attention. "How much?"

He shrugged. "A few hundred dollars since I've known her. What's the big deal? It's my money."

"Angela, if you want to be here, then let me ask the questions." Matt gave her a stern look before transferring his attention back to Dakota. "Why doesn't Heather ask her foster mother for money if she needs it? Why does she need so much?"

"She told me that she's supposed to be looking for a job and that each time she goes home without cash, she gets hit. She said it would be worse if anyone found out she spent her time with me instead of earning money." He gave a big sigh. "I've often wondered what kind of a job Ms. Forbes thinks she can get at night."

Angela gasped. "Your friend is a prostitute!" She tapped him on the head with a manicured fingernail. "If she's with you, a non-paying person," the look she gave him said he'd better be non-paying, "then, she goes home empty handed. You're a naive sap, son."

He shook his head. "No. She isn't like that. Matt?"

Without showing expression, Matt glanced up from his notes. "We're trying to find out exactly what goes on in that house. I won't speculate at this time."

Dakota crossed his arms and flounced back in his chair. "This sucks. I really like her."

"Look at how she dresses, son." Angela shook her head.

"You have a skirt exactly like one of hers." He laid his folded arms on the table and rested his head. "I don't think you should judge based on her clothes."

I stifled a grin and turned my head so Wayne couldn't see me laughing at his girlfriend. My sister did have a certain style associated with the oldest profession in the book. Mom and I had given up on her a long time ago. Maybe her son's words would get through to her.

Matt gave Angela another stern look. "Strike two."

"Whatever." She leaned back in her chair.

"Dakota, has Heather said anything to you about what happens in her home? Who comes and goes? Why she's expected to be out at night?"

"No. She sneaks out at night because she hates it there. That's all I know. Can I go now? I have school tomorrow and want to go see Brian afterward."

Good idea. Hopefully, the young man would be awake by tomorrow afternoon.

"Yes. If I have more questions, I'll stop by." Matt stood. He cast a dejected look at the mirror.

Poor man. He would've loved being able to wrap up his case with a few well-worded questions. Unfortunately, I believed Dakota. He didn't know anything. That didn't mean he wasn't trying to find information, though. That was for sure. After all, he'd hired me to find out what was going on with Heather. Now, there were other girls to worry about. I felt very inadequate for the task. What if I failed this time?

"Ready to go home?" Matt entered the room. "Wayne will give us a ride to my car."

Fatigue weighed on me like wet wool blankets. "I'm more than ready to go home."

It was still after midnight by the time we retrieved Matt's car and pulled onto my street. I leaned forward as we pulled into the driveway. The front door stood open. No lights burned in the house. "Did you set the alarm when we left?"

"I never forget, but Angela does every time. Stay here." He retrieved a Glock from his glove compartment.

There was no way I was staying in the car alone. I bolted from the vehicle and followed close on his heels. Mom's van sat in its usual spot. My heart froze. "Mom's home." I pulled my pink nine-millimeter from my purse and clutched it in a sweaty palm.

"For heaven's sake, don't shoot me," Matt hissed when he noticed my gun.

"I don't plan on it." *Please, God, don't let me mess up and kill the man I love.*

We stepped into my pitch black foyer. "Sadie?" I said in a loud whisper. The last time someone broke into my home, my dog was locked in my bedroom, and the cats in the pantry. I wouldn't care if they were locked in the closet, so long as they were unharmed.

"Sadie?" Tears stung my eyes when I didn't hear an answering whimper or bark.

"Shh." Matt put a hand on my arm.

We stiffened at a creak of floorboards overhead.

"Who else is home?"

"Cherokee, maybe."

He handed me his phone. "Call Wayne. Tell him to keep Angela and Dakota at the station, but for him to come."

I nodded and punched in his number, then whispered as quietly as possible what Matt had said. Wayne promised to be there in five minutes. By this time, Matt was heading up the stairs and disappearing in the dark, leaving me alone in the foyer.

A sound to my left had me whirling in the direction of the kitchen. Should I check it out or stay by the front door where I could run out if danger threatened? No. If I didn't make sure it wasn't an intruder, they might sneak up on Matt and harm him. I couldn't let that happen.

I took a deep breath of courage and tiptoed through the arch leading to the kitchen. Why did it always seem as if things happened on nights of a full moon? I could barely make out the shape of the counters or the refrigerator.

A door creaked to my right. I whirled and pulled the trigger. Oh!

"Heavens to Betsy!" A form crumpled to the floor.

"Mom?" Oh, God, I shot my mother.

"Stormi?" Matt called from upstairs.

"I killed her!" Tears blurred my vision.

Hands slapped mine away as I felt around my mother's body. "You missed, fool. Turn on the light."

"You aren't dead?"

"Seriously?"

I jumped to my feet and flicked on the light. Mom was very much alive and angry. I couldn't say the same for the basement door. A big hole showed what a poor aim I'd been.

"It was an accident. My hand was sweaty. I thought it was someone coming through the back door." I sagged into a chair and held my gun out. "Someone take this for everyone's safety."

Matt removed the weapon and placed it on the counter. "Anne?"

"I'm fine." She had a hand over her heart. "Other than a mild heart attack. Oh, Robert." She pounded down the basement stairs.

I raised my gaze to Matt's questioning glance and shrugged. I no longer tried to figure out why my family did what they did. Although, it was surprising that Mom had a man stay the night. A few minutes later, a very much awake looking Robert Smithfield climbed the stairs. Thank goodness, he still wore his suit.

"I fell asleep on the sofa. What a way to get woken up."

"I left him there," Mom said, tightening the sash of her robe. "Then, I heard people walking around up here. I thought it was the kids. It's much too late for them to be awake."

Cherokee entered the kitchen wearing short shorts and a big tee shirt, and clutching Ebony. "I heard a bang."

"Your aunt tried to shoot me," Mom said. "Go back to bed."

"I said it was an accident." I spoke to Mom, but glared at Robert, whose eyes almost bugged of his head at the sight of my sleepy, but beautifully exotic niece. "Time for everyone who doesn't live here to go, and the rest of us to get to bed." I stood up and placed two hands on Robert's back, pushing him toward the back kitchen door. "Good night." I shoved him out and slammed the door.

"What has gotten into you?" Mom yanked the door open. "Call me later," she told Robert.

"I didn't like the way he was looking

at Cherokee." I sat back down.

"Gross." My niece whirled and thundered back up the stairs. "Sadie's on my bed."

After she left the room, Matt pulled a sheet of paper from his pocket. "This was taped to your bathroom mirror."

"What's going on?" Wayne, followed closely by Angela and Dakota, raced into the room. "Sorry. They refused to stay behind."

"We have no control over this family," Matt said.

I read the note in my hand out loud. "Don't think about getting involved. Write your love stories and mind your own business. Learn from past attempts on your life. This time, you might not be as lucky." I opened my fingers to let the paper flutter to the floor.

I'd done what Matt asked and not gotten openly involved. Why the threat? I wasn't snooping and asking questions.

"Not setting the alarm is completely irresponsible." I glared at Angela. "Mom could have been murdered."

"By you," Mom said. "No one else

tried to shoot me. Still, Angela, you need to remember to set the alarm. Cherokee was home, too."

"I was distraught!" She planted fists on her spandexed hips. "Dakota's friend was beaten up, my son was being questioned by the police, and he needed his mother."

"I'm going to bed." Dakota grabbed a cookie out of the cookie jar and clomped upstairs.

"I'm going back to work." Wayne clapped Matt on the shoulder. "You deal with all…" he waved a hand toward us.

"Impossible." He leaned forward and kissed me, then picked up the typed note. "Things look fine here. I'll see you in a few hours."

I nodded and wiped the back of my hand across my face. "I know. Don't go anywhere alone." It was becoming second nature to never be alone because of outside threats.

He laughed and left, setting the alarm and closing the front door

"I'm going back to bed." Mom patted my shoulder. "Try not to kill me in my sleep."

"Very funny." I eyed my gun with distaste. Maybe some classes on gun safety was in my future.

I made the rounds, checking windows and locking doors. I thought about fetching Sadie from my niece's room, but the scaredy-cat dog was safer there than with me. Danger followed me like Hansel and Gretal after bread crumbs, and I was getting too old for nursery rhymes. It was time to find something else to disrupt my life.

9

Sleep took a lot of time coming. By the time my eyes closed, the sun was peeking through the curtains. I groaned and pulled the pillow over my head. The day could wait.

"Aunt Stormi?" Dakota's loud whisper cut through the pillow. "I know you aren't sleeping. I heard you tossing and turning."

"Go away."

"I need to talk to you." He yanked the pillow away from my face. "I wasn't completely honest with Matt."

That got my attention. I sprang to a sitting position and scooted against the headboard. "Go on."

He perched on the edge of the mattress and took a deep breath. "Heather gave me this. I'm really scared." He handed me a photo. "She said that her and the other girls are trapped. If they tell anyone, they'll disappear and be labeled runaways."

"Yet she told you." I took the picture. My heart stopped. Smiling up at a handsome boy was Cherokee.

"There's more." He handed me pictures of her at work, arriving home, and on dates. "Heather says they're after my sister."

"Who are they?" I put the pictures in a pile and grabbed my cell phone to call Matt.

"I don't know. That's what I need you to find out."

"I'm not the police. I'm a writer who writes about the trouble she gets into. This is over my head."

He reached for the phone. "You can't call Matt. If they find out we went to the authorities, they'll know Heather told me."

"Matt is discreet." I held it out of his reach. "This is serious stuff, Dakota."

He glared. "What kind of investigator are you? Fine!" He stood. "I'll keep looking on my own. Whatever happens is on your head." He stormed from the room, leaving me with my finger poised over the buttons of my phone.

The right thing to do was to call Matt. So, why wasn't I pressing the buttons? I sagged back against my pillows. Because I was in the proverbial space between a rock and a hard place. If I called him, I risked putting teenage girls, and my nephew, in danger. If I didn't call, my niece might disappear and be sold to some disgusting pervert old enough to be her grandfather. I pressed the buttons. I'd deal with the aftermath later. Family came first.

"Hello." I expected the raspy voice of having woken Matt. Instead, he sounded alert, as if he'd been awake for hours.

"I need you."

"Words every man wants to hear." He chuckled.

"No, seriously. Cherokee is in trouble."

"On my way." Click.

I climbed from bed and dressed in jeans and a tee shirt. I really need variation in my wardrobe. Slipping my feet into ballet flats, I followed the scent of brewing coffee to the kitchen.

Mom and Angela nursed cups in front of them. I tossed the pictures on the table. "Where's Cherokee?"

"Upstairs. Oh, my, gosh!" My sister grabbed the photos. "What are these? What are you not telling me? Cherokee!" She raced from the room and up the stairs as fast as stilettos would allow.

She thundered back down as Matt barged through the door a few minutes later. Angela grabbed the collar of his dress shirt. "My daughter is gone."

He peered over her shoulder at me and peeled her hands off his shirt. "Come to the table. Dakota!"

A very sullen Dakota joined us. He glanced at me as if I were a traitor. "Family is more important than friends."

"You knew something like this would happen?" Angela shrieked at him.

"Calm down. We don't know that anything has happened. Stormi, fill me in." Matt poured himself a cup of coffee and sat at the table.

I showed him the photos and told him what little Dakota had said that morning. I watched as his face hardened.

He slipped the photos into his shirt pocket. "Could she be at work? Anne, would you call them? Angela and Dakota, start calling her friends. Let's rule out every possibility before jumping to conclusions."

As everyone rushed to do their assigned jobs, I leaned closer to Matt. "You don't believe she's at work, do you?"

"She could be."

"The store doesn't open for two more hours." I grabbed a napkin and started shredding it into tiny pieces on the table. My heart knew she wasn't at work. She might have left for work, but she won't have made it.

"She didn't show," Mom said. "She was supposed to be there fifteen minutes ago to prepare to open. She's never late for work. What do we do?"

"I'm calling it in, and heading over to talk to Carol Forbes. This is gone on long enough." He pushed back from the table and marched out, me chasing behind.

"Go back," he said. "This isn't a job for you."

"I'll stay back when you approach the house. Please. It's my niece."

He sighed and nodded, sliding behind the wheel of his truck. Seconds later, we peeled rubber roaring down the street. Matt was out of the truck and marching up the walk to Carol's house before I got out.

"They moved." Rusty popped up from the bushes. "In the dark."

"What? Matt!" I grabbed Rusty's arm and pulled him from his hiding place. "When? Before midnight or after?"

"Rusty don't know."

"What's going on?" Matt jogged to my side.

"Rusty said they moved out."

"Yeah, I could tell through the window. The house is empty."

Tears blurred my vision. "Do you think they took Cherokee?"

"I don't know. We need to talk to this boyfriend of hers."

We hurried back to the truck and sped

toward the strip mall on the outskirts of town. Cherokee worked at a clothing store that catered to teens. The place was locked up tight.

Matt pounded on the door until a little mouse of a girl with coke bottle glasses opened the door. "We're closed," she said.

"Not for us." Matt flashed his badge.

"Oh." She stepped back. "I'm the only one here. Normally, I only work in the back. I'm not the norm for customers, but no one showed up today."

Matt pulled out the picture of Cherokee and her boyfriend. "Do you know these people?"

"Sure. That's Cherokee and Jon. They work here. She didn't show up this morning. He isn't scheduled until tomorrow." The poor thing's hands shook as if she were being interrogated.

"I need an address for Jon."

She glanced from Matt to me. "Can I call my boss?"

"No," Matt said. "Get me the address, then you can do whatever you want."

"Yes, sir." She scurried to a back room, the two of us following, and opened a drawer in a metal file cabinet. "Jon is new. Stays to himself mostly." She pulled an application from a file and made a quick copy of a page inside, then handed it to Matt. "Is he in trouble? Or Cherokee? Some lady called this morning—"

Matt smiled. "Thank you. You've been a big help." He turned and headed back outside.

"Lock the door," I told the girl before following him. "If you see Cherokee, tell her to call her aunt."

Seconds later, we once again sped down the road, this time to an apartment complex. I knew without Matt saying a word, that it was a waste of our time. Still, we couldn't leave any stone unturned. We had to follow every lead.

The woman whose door Matt pounded on had something to talk about for a month. Despite her protests that no young man lived there, we searched the small crocheted doily-covered place.

Matt handed her a business card, expressed his apology for disturbing her day, and stormed from the apartment. "I'm taking you home now. I need to go back undercover for a few days." He glanced at me as we got in the car. "I won't be around. Please, please, be careful."

I nodded. "I'll be looking for my niece. You be careful."

He slid his hand behind my head and pulled me close. "Keep your gun and Tazer close at all times." He claimed my lips roughly, almost as if he thought it might be the last kiss we gave each other.

When someone pounded on the truck window, telling us to get a room, we pulled apart. Matt started the ignition and backed from the parking spot.

The drive back to my house was made in silence. When we'd parked again, this time leaving the engine running, Matt gripped the steering wheel so tightly, I thought he might snap it in half.

"I love you." I blinked back tears. "Try and find time to call."

He nodded. "I love you, too."

I exited the truck and stood on the lawn as he backed out and drove away. Why did it feel as if we'd said goodbye? I couldn't stop the tears from rolling down my cheeks as I headed for the kitchen.

Mom glanced up from where she sat, still holding a cup of coffee. "It's cold. I can heat some more if you'd like."

"No, thank you." I sat across from her. "Where's Angela and Dakota?"

"They decided to visit her friends in person. Mary Ann is in your office doing research on child trafficking." Her voice cracked. "Since she recently turned eighteen, does she count as a child?"

"I don't know." I swept the pile of napkin pieces I'd torn earlier into my hand, then, rather than get up and throw them away, let them fall back to the table top. "What do you think about the party we're catering on Friday?"

"What do you think?"

I exhaled sharply. "I think we should do it. It's tied up with all this. I just haven't figured out how."

She reached across the table and gripped my hand. "What are we going to do? This isn't me or you being taken this time."

"I know." I needed to come up with a plan, and fast.

"It's weird that Cherokee was taken," Mary Ann said, joining us at the table. "There was an episode in Little Rock, similar to what's happening here. The only girls involved were runaway and foster kids. Those considered disposable. The girls were rescued during a sports event, but those in charge were never caught." She tossed some printed papers on the table. "My guess … they came here. Now, they've gone somewhere else."

"How can we keep them from going farther than we can reach?" I drummed my fingers on the table. "What type of men frequent these…?"

"I don't know what they're called either. The girls don't appear to be sold, just bought for a time." Mary Ann shook her head slowly. "The prime age is fifteen to nineteen. Who do we know that could go undercover as a lost girl?"

"You."

"Either one of you could, actually." Mom tilted her head. "With the proper clothes and makeup, you could do it. You'd have to wear a wig. That red hair is a dead giveaway."

We'd all lost our minds, clutching at straws in desperation. "Let's see what happens on Friday night first, okay? I also want to talk to Norma some more. So much has been happening, I haven't been able to check in with her to see what Tyler found out. And…there's Tyler's friend to question."

"All of which I will handle." Wayne strolled into the kitchen as if he were a part of the family and tossed a box of doughnuts onto the table. "Door was unlocked and the alarm not set. Guess y'all didn't learn anything last night." He grinned. "Yes, Matt told me. He also asked me to keep an eye on you. Mary Ann's squeeze is holding down things at the office."

"Short of arresting me," I said, glaring, "you can't stop me from trying to find Cherokee."

"I will arrest you if I have to." He opened the box and pulled out an éclair. "But, I'm in agreement that we need a woman on the inside."

My mouth fell open. I almost died on

the spot. Wayne Jones agreed with me. "Aren't you worried about what Matt will say?"

"Nah. I can take him. We've been talking about the same thing, just not the idea of using his sister and girlfriend. But, for lack of anyone else, you'll do. When can we do this?"

"Give me a few days." I had a party to get through and a former prostitute turned friend to coerce into helping.

10

After a day of aimlessly drifting through the motions of being a successful author and conjuring up horrible images of my niece at the hands of evil men, I now flipped through television channels with the speed of time. My next step depended on whether my gut feelings about Bomberg's party was correct. If I was wrong, I wasn't sure going undercover as a teenage girl would work. Either way, it was most likely the dumbest idea I'd ever gotten involved in.

I was twenty-eight years old. Who was going to believe me to be nineteen?

The ringing of the doorbell pulled me out of my musings. I tossed the remote control on the sofa and answered the door.

Rusty reached inside and yanked me out. "Light is on."

"Okay." I frowned. "Maybe because I'm still awake?"

"At foster house." He whirled and leaped off the porch.

"Sadie, we're going jogging!" I grabbed her leash off a hook by the door.

"Not without me." Mom handed me a beanie. "Cover that beacon of a head of yours. Do I have time to change into dark clothes?"

"No." I sighed. The last time Mom went with me to check out a house, she'd insisted we dress all in black like a couple of spies. "We're going to pretend we're jogging. We can't wait."

She slipped her feet into Keds. "Ready."

I did the same with a pair of my niece's Converses, and choked back tears, hoping, praying, she'd get to wear them again. I clipped the leash to Sadie's collar, grabbed a flashlight from the foyer table, and raced outside to follow Rusty, who was already halfway to Carol's former house.

"Wait." Mom thrust my purse at me when she caught up.

"No one takes their purse jogging."

"It has your gun and Tazer."

Right. I slung the purse over my shoulder and kept running. By the time we reached the corner, we were both panting for breath.

"Maybe a more gentle job?" Mom bent over at the waist.

"Definitely. Come on." I grabbed her arm.

"I'm going to die." She groaned and followed.

When we reached the house in the cul de sac, Rusty hunched behind some bushes. "Light still there."

"Great. Stay here and whistle if someone comes."

His face scrunched. "Like a bird?"

"Yes. Exactly like that."

"What kind of bird?"

"Any bird, Rusty." I sighed, handed him Sadie's leash, and grabbed Mom's hand, hoping that if he actually whistled, I would be able to tell the difference between him and a feathered friend.

With Mom's hand firmly in mine, I made my way to the big front window and peered through a crack in the curtains. Sure enough, the beam of a flashlight bobbed around the room. I reached over and slowly turned the doorknob. Locked.

"We'll have to go around back," I whispered.

"Let go of my hand and get your gun out."

I liked holding her hand. I knew where she was and didn't feel as scared. "What if I shoot you?"

"Please don't." She scooted around the corner of the house.

I dug my gun out of my purse and duck-walked after her, only standing straight when I passed the window. I thought of calling Wayne, but what if it were nothing more than kids goofing around in a vacant house? I'd rather he spent his time searching for Cherokee, than chasing wild geese down the proverbial trail.

"Kitchen door is open." Mom's hoarse whisper sounded abnormally loud.

"Get behind me." I stepped in front of her. Holding my weapon in both hands, I stepped over the threshold and into a room lit only by a moon playing hide-n-go-seek with the clouds. I didn't dare turn on my flashlight and give away our presence.

Mom stepped on the back of my heel. I scowled and moved forward. This was the queen of bad ideas.

"What are they looking for?" She asked. "The house is empty."

"I don't know. Hush."

"Maybe Carol forgot something and came back."

"In the name of heaven, be quiet." We moved to the arch leading from the kitchen to the dining room, then into the living room. These big, old Victorians had loads of hiding places even when empty. Arched doorways, curved walls, hidden rooms. My finger itched to rest on the trigger of the gun.

A muffled thud sounded from a room down the hall. The nighttime visitor had moved from the living room to one of the bedrooms. I clicked on my flashlight for a moment and shined it around the empty living room. The beam highlighted a white scrap of fabric on the floor.

"That's Robert's handkerchief." Mom

scooped it up. "He did say he planned on paying Carol a visit. Something about her bank account."

"I guess she didn't want to take it with her." I flicked off the light.

Mom stuffed the handkerchief into her pocket.

A curse drifted down the hall, sending us ducking against the wall. The pounding of footsteps coming down the hall sent my pulse into overdrive. I peeked around the corner and spotted someone in dark clothes heading up the stairs. When they reached the top and disappeared into a room, I waved Mom forward.

On tiptoes, we dashed up the stairs and into a large bedroom. "Be ready to duck into the closet," I said.

"The balcony would be better. We'd be trapped in the closet."

Good thinking. The person was searching for something. They were bound to look in the closet. All I needed was one good look at their face and we could leave.

"Go!" Mom shoved against me.

We raced for the balcony as footsteps

neared. I fumbled with the latch, finally getting the door open. We jumped outside and I closed the door, each of us taking refuge on each side of the door. A simple glance outside might not reveal our presence, but if the person were to step outside…

The lock on the door engaged.

I gaped, wide-eyed at Mom. "Now what?"

"You're the private investigator. You tell me." She leaned over the railing. "It's a long way down."

One story was too far to jump. I studied the nearby oak tree. If we could reach the nearest branch…

"Look." Mom pointed to where a man, dressed in black, carried a small cardboard box around the corner of the house.

In the distance, came the sounds of a whippoorwill. Good boy, Rusty. Of course, that particular bird wasn't common around Oak Meadows Estates.

A car door slammed. I cupped my hands around my mouth. "Rusty! Sadie!"

An answering bark sent my hope

soaring. We would get off the balcony in no time.

Rusty stared up at us. "Want a ladder?"

"Yes, please."

"Be back soon." He told Sadie to stay and left.

When he hadn't returned thirty minutes later, I knew he'd forgotten. I eyed the tree again.

I handed Mom the gun, then dumped my purse on the floor of the balcony. Holding onto the strap, I swung it toward the tree. On the fifth attempt, I snagged the tree branch. "Easy. Now, all we have to do is grab a hold of the branch and jump. It should lower us gently to the ground."

"Are you crazy?" Mom's eyes widened.

"It worked when I was a kid. Angela and I jumped off the catwalk on the swing set this same way."

"You were a lot smaller back then."

"You go first. Then, I'll snag the branch again and go after you."

"Wonderful." She planted her fists on

her hips. "If I die, I'm coming back to haunt you." She closed her eyes. The silent moving of her lips told me she was praying. Good. We would need the help of God's angels.

She opened her eyes and climbed over the balcony. Holding on with one hand, she reached out for the other. "I'll have to give a little jump."

"Want me to push you?"

She squeaked and swatted at me. "Don't you dare. If I fall and break something, go ahead and put me out of my misery."

"You aren't a horse I can just put down, Mom."

The flash of a bulb alerted me to the fact we were no longer alone. I peered down at my neighbors, the Salazars.

"You're back," I said, smiling. "And making the rounds."

"We didn't expect to see you and your mother on the balcony of a home that doesn't belong to you," Tony said. "Need some help? Jump. I'll catch you." He laughed and slapped his leg as if he'd said the funniest thing in the world. He was always making jokes in reference to his "little people" status.

His wife, Becky, slapped his shoulder. "Stop it. This is not the time for jokes. We should call someone."

"Stormi wants me to jump," Mom said.

"That's not a good idea." Tony shook his head, still laughing. "I'll call the handyman."

"Rusty left to get a ladder a while ago." I leaned against the railing. "Maybe you could find him?"

The railing wobbled, screeched, and broke free as the cement under our feet gave way. Mom and I screamed and grabbed for the tree branch. It let us down all right. We plummeted to the ground faster than I had as a child. The wind left my lungs in a whoosh as Mom landed on top of me.

"Well," she said, her nose inches from mine. "That wasn't as bad as I thought."

"Speak…for…yourself." I shoved her off me and did a mental check to see if anything was broken.

"Ann?" Robert helped her off me. "What in the world is going on?"

"Just some friendly neighborhood scouting." She held down her hand to help me up. "What are you doing here?"

"We had a coffee date." His eyes narrowed. "When I got to your house, I found that Rusty fellow lugging a ladder. He told me you were here."

At least Rusty would have made it back eventually. I gathered up what I could find from my emptied purse, shoved the contents back inside, and gripped the now torn strap. "I'm going home."

I grabbed Sadie's leash and limped toward home, having hurt my left ankle when I fell. What a waste of time. We didn't know the identity of the intruder or what he had found in Carol's house.

"I think I will accompany you to the party on Friday," Robert told Mom behind me. "You tend to get in trouble when left to your own devices."

"Only because I follow Stormi."

Gee, thanks, Mom. I didn't recall inviting her along. What did Robert think he was going to do? Enjoy a free meal on someone else while pretending to be a caterer? He'd never shown interest in Mom's delectables before. At least not the kind she baked.

I grinned evilly. I'd think of something he could do to help us. "That's a great idea. We'll need someone on garbage patrol." I glanced over my shoulder. "You won't mind, will you? It would be a big help."

"Please, say yes, Robert." Mom put a hand on his arm. "Otherwise, Stormi will make me do it. There's no way she can take out the garbage in the dress she bought."

He didn't look pleased, but he nodded. "Anything to help out the ladies."

Wonderful. Maybe he wasn't so bad after all. Mom seemed to think him the greatest thing since dishwashers. I still hadn't decided if he was good enough to replace my Dad.

When we got home, I headed to my room and started a warm bath. Hopefully, the hot water would soothe my aches and pains. But, nothing would ease the grief over Cherokee's disappearance, or my worry over Matt, other than seeing them standing safe and sound in front of me.

11

My stomach didn't contain fluttering butterflies, it corralled stampeding elephants. I placed a hand on my flat midrift in a vain attempt to still the beasts as I glanced over a large warehouse transformed into a millionaire's party house.

In a few minutes, the glittering place would fill with people in formal dress. People who wanted to taste Mom's baking. Here I stood, looking better than I thought possible, and feeling ill.

"Here." Mom thrust a glass of pale gold champagne in my hands. "It'll settle your nerves."

"I don't drink."

"Just sip it. I'm not asking you to

guzzle the stuff. You need your wits about you."

Did I ever. I took a sip of the bubbly, surprisingly tasty drink. I wouldn't want to make a habit of it, but an occasional glass in celebration might not be too bad. "I'm going to wander a bit."

"That's what you're here for." Mom frowned. "I'm the one hired to stay behind the table."

I smiled. She might be hired help, but she was one of the most beautiful women in the place. The flowing pantsuit she wore suited her small frame. She wore her red hair, only a shade darker than my own, in an elegant French twist. It wasn't hard to see why Robert seemed smitten with her.

Speaking of Robert. The man downed a liquid from a whiskey glass and ducked down a hallway flanked by two men with bulging muscles.

When I approached them, they moved closer together. "What's down there?" I asked.

"Men's restroom. Women's is over there." One of them motioned his head across the room.

"Can't I just look around?" I tried peering between them and came up against a solid wall of flesh. "I'd love to see what they've done with the place."

"Go the other way, ma'am."

I sighed, not bothering to try and flirt. Tweedle Dee and Tweedle Dum wouldn't know a good-looking woman in a tight dress if she kissed them. I made my way back to Mom and spent the next few minutes setting out the desserts.

Mr. Bomberg approached the table and snatched a bite-sized cheesecake square off a crystal plate. "This looks fabulous ladies. While I hired you to serve, please take time to enjoy yourself." His eyes raked over me. "You, I want to mingle and flirt with the men."

I almost choked on the next sip of champagne. "That's not what I was hired for. If you want decorations, you'll need to order them."

A muscle ticked in his right cheek. "My guests expect lovely scenery. You, my dear, rank up there with the best. I insist you mingle." He gave me a smile reminiscent of a shark right before one took the bite out of someone's leg, then turned and sauntered down the very hall Robert had disappeared into.

By now, several more guests had arrived, mostly men, but some finely dressed women hung on a few arms. Men outnumbered the women five to one. And every single man went to the restroom for at least thirty minutes shortly upon arrival, leaving their eye candy to sit alone on plush sofas.

Robert returned, straightening his tie, and grinning like a child who got a new toy. "Quite the shindig Bomberg puts on, isn't it?"

"I suppose." I set my empty champagne flute on a tray. "How is the men's room?"

He laughed. "You're a strange woman, Stormi Nelson. Come." He crooked his arm at me and winked at Mom. "Let me escort the second most beautiful woman around the room. Perhaps I can drum up business for the bank. This looks like a wealthy lot."

"I should stay and help Mom."

"Nonsense," she said. "Go with Robert."

I sighed and slipped my arm through his. Of course, Mom would be thrilled. She wanted nothing more than for me to get to know her boyfriend better. Unfortunately, my heart hadn't fully healed from Dad's murder. Not enough for another man to step into his place.

Robert introduced me to person after person as the best-selling author, Stormi Nelson, daughter of his girlfriend. I kept a smile plastered on my face and tried to look interested when, in actuality, I studied the face of every man I came into contact with. The few women with them must have thought my intense study a form of flirtation and sent dirty looks my way.

They could relax. Not a man there could hold a candle to Matt.

Robert stopped our circle around the room a few feet away from the guarded hall entrance. A small man in a wrinkled suit tried to push between the two muscle men.

"Let me pass," he said. "You can't

discriminate."

"You're credit with us is bad, Mr. Worth."

I dubbed the talking muscle man Tweedle Dee. The other had yet to say a word all night.

"I'm good for it, I tell you."

"Excuse me." Robert removed my arm and put a hand on the small man's shoulder. "Come with me, Frank. There's nothing back there for you." He led the man away, leaving me staring at a brick wall between two men as stalwart as cement posts.

I was starting to think there was more down that hallway than a simple men's bathroom. I turned and headed for the women's room. Maybe I'd find answers there.

The opposite hallway was lit by bare bulbs hanging on cords from the ceiling. Obviously, the grandeur of the party didn't extend further than the main room. I followed the brick-walled, cement floor hall to a door with a handwritten sign stating simply "Women". I pushed the door open and stepped into a room containing nothing more than a toilet and a sink.

I took care of business, washed my hands, and exited the room. Rather than head back to the party, I turned right and followed the hall around a corner. Blocking the way was another muscle man. This one looked as if he might have been the model for Mr. Clean.

He had his back to me. I stepped back around the corner and leaned against the wall.

I needed a plan to get past him. I rushed back to the dessert table and grabbed another champagne.

Mom's eyebrows rose. "Still nervous?"

"Camouflage." I grinned.

"I'm glad to see you enjoying yourself." A warm breath tickled the back of my neck.

I turned and came nose-to-nose with Mr. Bomberge. I moved back as far as the table would allow.

"I've had several men comment on your beauty," he said. "Many of them are interested in spending time with you, despite your more…advanced age."

"I'm not even thirty! That's hardly old age."

"Compared to the other women here, it is. Of course, you do look amazingly young for your age." He started to caress my cheek, then, apparently growing a brain, dropped his hand.

"Thank you." I think.

I stared around the room some more. He was right. If I looked close enough, the women couldn't be more than twenty. The fancy clothes, makeup, and stylish hair made them appear older. Most of the men they were with looked old enough to be their fathers or grandfathers. My stomach churned all over again. I faced Mr. Bomberg. Spiders skittered up and down my spine.

This was the type of man I'd have to deal with when I went undercover as a much younger girl. Could I handle it? Could I pretend to enjoy the attention? There was no time like the present to find out.

I gave Mr. Bomberg my most seductive look and trailed a finger down the sleeve of his suit jacket. "Sadly, you're the only man here I'm interested in."

Mom coughed. A piece of cookie flew across the table and landed on the floor at my feet.

"Let's go somewhere a bit more…private," I suggested. "Surely, there must be such a room in this big old warehouse."

"Of course, there—" A shout from down the men's hall diverted him from finishing his sentence. He chucked me under the chin. "We'll finish this conversation when I return." He hurried away.

As Robert rushed toward our table, I grabbed my champagne and headed back to the women's hallway. I felt a bit like an episode of Scooby Doo with characters running here and there.

The moment I neared the corner past the restroom, I pretended to stumble, sloshing champagne over my hand. "Excuse me," I slurred. "I've lost my way." I fell into Mr. Clean. His strong arms held me upright. "Oh." I trailed my dripping fingers down his cheek. "You're so massive."

"Miss, you can't be down here."

"I'm lost." I pouted, hoping I looked as alluring as I needed to be. "Can't you help me?"

More shouts emanated from the main room. Mr. Clean glanced over my shoulder, then propped me against the wall. "Stay here." He held out his hand as if commanding a dog.

"I'll stay if you promise to come back." I blew him a kiss. Then, the moment he disappeared around the corner, I kicked off my shoes and sprinted down the hall.

The farther I got, the dirtier and dingier the walls and floor. I'd had no idea such a place existed outside Oak Meadows. Life continued to point out my naivety.

I rounded a corner, only to jump back when I spotted two men beating the dickens out of a third. Each pound of fist against flesh made me cringe.

The third man looked up. "That all you got?"

I gasped and peered around the

corner, recognizing the voice of my beloved. Oh, why had I left my purse under the dessert table? If I ever needed my gun, now was the time.

Kicks joined the punches. I cried out, clamping my hand over my mouth as Matt's gaze collided with mine. He shook his head and I pulled back, tears streaming down my face. When I looked again, they were gone.

I dropped my glass, lifted my dress to my knees and ran. A large metal door hung open at the end of the corridor. Idling in front of the door was a white panel van with the words, Worth's Automotive painted on the side.

The two brutes lifted a limp Matt and tossed him in the back of the van. Without a glance in my direction, they slammed the doors closed, pitching me into darkness. I heard the roar of the van's engine as it pulled away.

I slid to the floor in a heap. Now, I'd not only lost my niece, but the man I loved. Where in the world did I begin to look for either one? I mentally took note of the name on the side of the van, linking the words with the short man removed from the party. I'd be looking him up at the first opportunity. Right now, I needed my purse and my cell phone so I could call Wayne.

I pushed to my feet. It wasn't until that moment that I realized the wall behind me was actually a door. A small slit in the door was at my eye level. I turned and stared through the opening. A form huddled against the wall. Long dark hair fell forward, obscuring the girl's face. "Cherokee?"

The girl didn't respond. Whether she was my niece or not, she needed my help. I rapped on the door. When she still didn't respond, I knocked harder. "Hello? Are you okay?"

Footsteps alerted me to someone coming. I stepped back from the door and resumed my drunken stagger, this time in the direction of the party room.

When I spotted Mr. Clean, I grinned. "You came back."

"Where are your shoes?"

"I have no idea." I held out a hand. "Carry me?"

A hit on the back of my head sent me to my knees. Darkness engulfed me.

12

I opened my eyes as Mr. Clean dropped me on a plush red sofa. "Who hit me?"

"No one." The look in his eyes chilled my blood. "You're drunk."

Mom glared down at me. "I told you not to have that second champagne."

"I didn't drink it." I struggled to a sitting position and put a hand to the back of my head. A hard knot rose under my fingers. "I've got a bump."

"You hit your head when you fell." Mr. Clean turned and stormed away.

"No, Mom, listen." I clutched her by the arm. "They took Matt away. They have a girl locked in a room." My throat clogged. Was Matt dead or alive? How long did he have if I didn't find him? I stood and waited for the dizziness to subside.

I had to get down the other hallway. There was way more than a concrete restroom attracting the men at the party. Where was my phone? I felt around my body, shoving my hand into my cleavage. I'd dropped it. No, it was in my purse.

I clutched my pounding head. "I need my purse."

"Sit." Mom lowered me back to the sofa. "Rest. People are leaving. I'll get Robert to help me clean up and then we'll discuss your shameful behavior."

"My purse. Please." I wiped the tears from my face with the palms of my hands, not caring if I smeared my makeup. My world was tumbling out of control, falling at my feet like dominoes.

The sight of Matt's battered face, the pained look in his eyes when he caught me watching, ripped at my gut. I felt every punch to his body. I still didn't know if the girl in the back room was my niece. She looked like her, but without seeing her face, how could I tell?

Mom handed me my purse. "There's no cell reception in here. Robert said it was because of the thick walls."

"I think they're holding Cherokee down that hall."

"What?" That got her attention.

"At least the girl looks like her. They have a girl locked in a room that looks like a jail cell."

Mom glanced toward the hall, then bent and peered into my eyes. "You aren't drunk?"

"No! I told you I didn't drink the second glass. It was strictly for camouflage."

"Ok. Pretend like you are to everyone. Even Robert. I'll get this mess cleaned up as fast as possible so we can contact Wayne."

Finally. If Mom believed me, it would be hard for anyone else not to. She could be very convincing. Why didn't she want Robert to know I was sober?

While I pondered the million questions roaming through my mind and increasing my worry over my loved ones, I watched as guests left and staff scurried to clean up. Robert and Bomberg huddled in a corner, casting glances my way. Let them think me a disgrace. The ache in my heart kept me focused on the task at hand; finding Matt and Cherokee.

What was taking Mom so long? I got to my feet, realizing I'd lost my new red shoes, and approached the table to start piling serving dishes into a plastic container. We worked without speaking. Her heart had to be as heavy as mine.

Once we were finished, Robert hefted one of the containers in his arms and led the way outside. Before we could get in the van, Mr. Clean jogged up.

"Your shoes." He handed me the red heels, and leaned close. "I'll do my best to keep him alive. Don't trust anyone." He straightened and hurried back into the building.

I glanced around, relieved to see that Mom and Robert were already in the van waiting for me. I climbed in the backseat. "This was an interesting evening."

"Especially for a gal who can't hold her champagne." Robert laughed, the oaf.

I shrugged and transferred my attention out the window. Let him think what he wanted to. His opinion didn't matter to me. Saving my family did. I pulled my cell phone from my purse and sent a text to Wayne, asking that he meet me at the house, but remain out of sight until I texted him the all clear.

I got an immediate response. Okay.

Relieved that I would have help, I allowed the tears to silently course down my cheeks. When we arrived at home, I wiped them away, grabbed a container of dishes from the back of the van, and turned to Robert. "Thank you for your help tonight, but we're very tired."

Mom gave me "the look". "I apologize for her rudeness." She gave him a quick kiss. "I'll talk to you in the morning."

"Goodnight, ladies." He flashed a grin and headed for his car parked across the street. Before he slid into the driver's seat, he waved. "Tomorrow."

"I need to break up with him." Mom returned his wave before unlocking the front door and turning off the alarm.

"Why? I thought you really liked him." I set the crate of dishes on the kitchen table.

She sighed. "I didn't like the way he

ogled the young women at that party. When a man professes love to me, I want to be the most beautiful woman in his eyes. Age shouldn't be a factor."

I hugged her. "I agree." I sent a text to Wayne to come in.

The backdoor opened. I screamed and clutched my throat. "Wayne Jones!"

"You told me to wait for the text. I did." He closed the door, then pulled the kitchen curtains closed. "What's up?"

As quickly as possible, I told him everything that occurred that night. His face hardened with every detail. "Let's go."

I slipped my feet into flats and grabbed my purse. Mom did the same. "We're ready," I said.

"In an evening gown?" Wayne asked.

"It isn't something I've never done before." I headed for the front door, meeting Angela on her way in.

She took one look at the three of us and declared she was coming along. "Where are we going?"

"To try and save Cherokee and Matt." I slid behind the wheel of my Mercedes.

Wayne took the front passenger seat, leaving Mom and my sister in the back. I turned the key in the ignition and sped toward the warehouse.

"You know they will have cleared out, right?" Wayne cut me a sideways glance.

"Yes. But they might have left clues."

"I was out walking the streets," Angela said, her voice barely loud enough to be heard. "No one has seen anything of my girl. Now, this might be the only lead we have. It's worth checking into."

"Agreed." We all said in unison.

Knowing I could trust, without a doubt, everyone in the car with me at that moment, I told Wayne about Mr. Clean's warning. "Do you think he's undercover?"

"Possibly." Wayne took his bottom lip between strong white teeth, then nodded. "Otherwise, you could very well have disappeared after being hit over the head. I'll see if I can find out who Mr. Clean is. For now, heed his advice. Don't trust anyone outside this car."

I was pretty sure I could trust Mary Ann. How could I possibly let her know about Matt?

Tears threatened again. I blinked them back. Now was the time for me to be strong. Even though I had plunged ahead with my sleuthing in the past, I always knew I had Matt's strong shoulder to lean on when I needed it. This time, he needed me. I wouldn't let him down.

The warehouse was dark when we arrived. No surprise there. I cut the engine and the lights on the car and the four of us silently exited the vehicle. Gravel crunched under our feet as we approached the front double doors. We stopped when we spotted the heavy steel lock.

"There's a back way. That's where they parked the van that took Matt." I lifted the hem of my dress and darted around the corner of the building.

A smaller lock hung on the back door. I pulled out my gun and shot it off before Wayne could stop me.

The door groaned as he slid it open. He pulled a small penlight from his pocket. "I'll go first." He unholstered his revolver and led the way. I entered second, then Angela, with Mom bringing up the rear.

"Give me your Tazer," Mom hissed. "I need some kind of a weapon. What if we run across a bad guy?"

I handed her the Tazer. Angela grabbed a piece of metal pipe from the floor. I doubted an armed man would be scared of us, but we might make someone think twice before shooting. I hoped.

"This is the room where I saw the girl." The door swung open at my touch. The cell was empty except for a bunk with a thin mattress.

"Where is she?" Angela darted forward. She stood in the center of the small room and turned in a circle. Her eyes filled with tears. "We're too late." She fell to her knees. The contact with the cement floor made a dull thud.

Mom stepped forward and wrapped her arms around her. "We'll find her."

"Wait." A glimmer in the corner of the room caught my attention. "Wayne, shine that light over here."

He did as I knelt in the dust. Blinking up at me was the silver purity ring I had given Cherokee. I picked it up. "It was her." I smiled. Cherokee might not have been fully conscious when I'd called out her name, but somehow she'd had the presence of mind to leave us a symbol of hope. I dropped it in Angela's outstretched hand.

I stepped into the dark corridor. Just a few feet from where I stood was where I'd last seen Matt. I closed my eyes against the image of his abuse.

"Are you okay?" Wayne stepped next to me.

"That's where Matt was beaten."

"He knew the danger when he accepted the assignment." He placed a hand on my shoulder. "Don't give up hope. Matt Steele lives up to his last name. He's tough."

I nodded. "I need to talk to Mary Ann."

"Let's take a quick look through the building, then we'll go."

Further searching revealed nothing new, other than another cement corridor with more cell like rooms. Only these rooms had mirrored windows rather than a slit in the door.

Wayne cursed. I glanced up in surprise. I'd never heard the big man utter a swear word before.

"What is it?" I asked.

"An auction."

I sagged against the wall. At least Cherokee hadn't been in this hall. "Why not my niece?"

"Maybe she isn't controlled yet." He grasped my arm and pulled me back to the others. "These types of *people* tend to drug their victims into submission before putting them up for sale."

"Oh, God." Angela turned and threw up in the corner.

Mom looked as if she might faint.

I wanted to throw up and faint. But, I had a job to do. I squared my shoulders and met Wayne's gaze. "What do we do now?"

"We visit Mary Ann." He moved to Angela's side and smoothed her hair from her face. "We'll find her, sweetheart." He pulled her to his chest in a rare public display of affection.

I turned away and made my way back to the car. By the time I started the engine, the others had joined me. The ride to Mary Ann's was made in silence.

Wayne exited the car first and pounded on the front door until a light inside flickered to life. When a sleepy Mary Ann answered the door, he stepped back. "Stormi needs to talk to you."

"Something happened to Matt." She fell into a porch rocker.

I sat in the chair next to her and gripped her hand. I told her everything I knew.

She took a ragged breath and lifted her eyes to mine. "When do we go undercover?"

13

I didn't try to be brave. Instead, I cried myself to sleep. The alarm rang too soon, startling me. I bolted upright, throwing my pillow toward the door. I wasn't quite sure what sort of weapon that might have been had my life been in danger, but it was the best my sleep-deprived brain could come up with.

"What are you doing?" A sleepy Mary Ann pulled her pillow over her face. As worried and distraught as myself, she hadn't wanted to return to the house she shared with her brother and opted to spend the night.

"Fighting off imaginary intruders." I flung off the blankets and shuffled to the adjoining bathroom.

A red-haired wraith stared back at me

from the mirror. Bloodshot eyes over bags enough to take on a week's vacation. If I were going to pass for nineteen, I needed a lot of work, and a foolproof plan. No more flying by the seat of my proverbial pants.

"We have to go shopping," Mary Ann called from the bedroom. "I don't have anything suitable for a teenage prostitute to wear."

"We're runaways." I pulled a brush through my hair.

"To be forced into prostitution." She leaned against the doorjamb. "I was a good girl in high school."

"Me, too." But, we were going to have to learn very quickly how to become troubled teens. "I want to visit a group home. Do you know of any?"

"Yes." Mary Ann breathed sharply through her nose. "It's a half hour drive from here. I'll call now."

I figured she might know of one, being Matt's sister and all. I pulled on a pair of baggy jeans, tied my hair back into a ponytail, and left on the tee shirt I'd slept in. Coffee mattered more than looking good at this point.

"Wayne." I stopped the moment I spotted him at the table. "I didn't expect to see you."

"Your mom offered me the guest room. I hope that's okay." He looked up from a steaming mug in front of him. "I wasn't comfortable leaving y'all alone."

"And I thank you for it." I made a beeline for the coffee pot. Bless the man for making a fresh pot.

"You look like hell."

"Gee, thanks. Just what every nineteen-year-old girl wants to hear." I poured my coffee, added a lot of white chocolate creamer, and joined him at the table. "Mary Ann and I are visiting a group home she knows. I need to see how troubled teens act."

"Sullen. Like the world hates them." He wrapped his big hands around the mug. "Angela is pretty torn up about her daughter. We need to find these people fast. If they sell her out of the country—"

"You don't have to tell me." Not to mention the longer Matt was gone, the less likely we'd find him alive.

"We're good to go," Mary Ann said,

entering the kitchen. "The girls will be having breakfast in half an hour. We can go after that."

"Good. That gives me time to make sure Angela is all right." Wayne pushed back from the table.

"You can't go with us." Mary Ann shook her head. "You scream cop. The girls won't talk to us if you're there."

"Then I'll wait in the van." He marched out of the room, his tone leaving no room for discussion.

I didn't mind. Knowing he was there would make me more comfortable.

On our prior ventures into crime-solving, I'd actually had fun. Even when my life was threatened. This time…there was nothing fun about it.

I stood up and moved to put my half-empty mug in the sink. Glancing out the kitchen window, I spotted Dakota slip something to Rusty. Then, the big man turned and jogged into the trees behind my property. I opened the back door. "Dakota!"

He shook his head. "Nothing gets past you, does it? Before you ask, I paid him ten dollars to wander around those empty warehouses down by the river. That seems like a good place to stash people."

"You're the smartest boy I know." I grabbed him in a hug. "Sheer genius."

"I told you I'm a good detective. When do we go?"

"Mary Ann and I have other plans this morning." I held him at arm's length. "But, when we do investigate those buildings, you aren't going with us. It's too dangerous. Rusty is like a ghost. Let's see if he finds anything suspicious before wasting our time there."

His face darkened and he pulled away. "I'm looking for my sister with you or without you. It's safer with you, isn't it?"

"Yes." I sighed. "I'll find something you can help us with."

"Maybe you and Mary Ann can hide in those buildings when you runaway." He grinned and moved past me. "Don't forget. I have a box of spy equipment. I hear everything you two say."

I'd forgotten about that stuff. "Are there cameras small enough to hide in jewelry?"

"Sure. Come on." He led the way to his room where he retrieved a box from under his bed. "I have a necklace and a ring with a camera. This one…" he held up a small round device, "fits in the end of a cigarette real good."

"We'll take the two jewelry pieces. Where do the images shoot back to?"

"Wherever I want. Wayne can watch on a laptop from here or in his car."

The costume jewelry was perfect. Not too gaudy. The necklace was a cross with a fake ruby in the center, which was the camera. The ring was shaped like a daisy with the camera in the center of the flower. "Yep. A genius." I flashed Dakota a grin and headed back downstairs to meet up with Mary Ann and Wayne.

I handed Mary Ann the necklace. "I feel a lot better about our plan now."

"Me, too." Wayne opened the front door, then stepped back while I set the alarm.

I cast a glance toward the kitchen, wondering whether Mom still slept or if she'd gone in to work. After the long night we'd had, I decided to let her be. I'd fill her and Greta in on our day later.

With Wayne driving, we made it to the group home in twenty-five minutes. I sat in the front passenger seat and studied the red-brick building that looked like a small town elementary school converted into a home. The conversion failed miserably. There wasn't anything homey about the place. Even the flowers out front dried up under the chill of fall.

The dead lawn crunched under our feet as we approached the iron gate over the front door. I pressed the bell.

"May I help you?" A voice came from a small speaker above the doorbell.

Mary Ann leaned close. "Mary Ann Steele and Stormi Nelson. We have an appointment." She turned to Wayne. "Wait in the car."

He sighed and headed back, clearly not happy with the order. But, to his credit, he didn't argue.

A loud click attracted our attention back to the gate. Seconds later, it swung open.

"Please close the gate upon entry.

You'll have to press another button to open the front door."

"Yes, ma'am." I felt as if I were stepping into a prison rather than a place some people called home.

Mary Ann didn't look disturbed in the slightest. Instead, she acted as if bars clanging shut behind her was a normal occurrence. There might be a lot more to my assistant than I'd had time to discover.

She pressed a larger button to the right of the double metal doors. They swung open and we stepped into what looked like the front office of a school. I was pretty certain my first assessment was correct, and we were in a converted school.

A woman glanced up from a computer behind a green metal desk. "Miss Steele?" Her eyes widened when she got to me. "Oh. *The* Stormi Nelson."

A fan and I had no makeup on and had dressed in little more than my pajamas. I grinned and offered my hand for a shake. "Nice to meet you."

"Are you doing research for a book?"

"Something like that."

"Let me ring the headmistress. Harriet Marshall has run this facility for almost twenty years. She's a marvel."

We waited, me glancing at runaway posters on the walls, until a squat woman with a military haircut approached us. "I'm Marshall. Nice to meet you."

"Mary Ann Steele, and I'm Stormi Nelson."

"Love your books." Her smile softened her look. She motioned her head toward the posters. "Seems like we lose a girl a month, no matter how careful we are with security. Let me introduce you two to some of our angels."

I was pretty sure the primary angel in that place was Harriet, but I kept my mouth shut. We strolled down a hall with classrooms being used as bedrooms. Belligerent faces glared at us as we passed. We ended up in a large room where tables, chairs, and sofas were used by a variety of ages between thirteen and eighteen. The clamor of twenty plus girls hushed when we entered.

Harriett clapped her hands. "My angels, we have a special visitor today. A famous author is here to do research. Please give her a warm welcome."

A few girls shrugged and returned to the television, another slapped her book closed and stormed past us, and a few more turned back to painting each others' nails. I chewed the inside of my lip and decided to try and talk to a lone girl in the corner who seemed bent on hiding behind a mane of blond hair.

"Hey." I sat next to her.

"Hey." Her sigh seemed to carry the weight of the world. "Here to stare at the homeless, are you? Well, get on with it."

"My name is Stormi."

"Lara."

"How old are you?"

"I'll be eighteen next month and sent packing."

Great. I had my example. Across the room, Mary Ann attempted to speak with her own non-talkative teen.

"Look, I'm not here to research. I need help." I leaned close and pretended to study a hole in the knee of my jeans. "My niece disappeared. She's about your age. I need to pretend to be your age so I can find her."

"Are you crazy?" She hissed, glancing toward the other girls. "People disappear and are never seen again. You want to go out there in that?"

"I have to. The same people took my boyfriend."

She closed her eyes and rested her head against the wall. "What's your plan? Your disguise?"

"Runaway?"

"Won't work. You're too old. Nobody cares if an eighteen-year-old runs away."

I guessed it wouldn't be any different for a nineteen-year-old. "I'm open for suggestions."

"You're a homeless drug addict peddling your body on the streets." She opened one eye. "You'll get grabbed for sure. Wear something slinky and act like you hate everyone unless a prospective John approaches. Then put on the charm. The right John will come along and you'll find your niece. Pray she's still alive."

"What are your plans when you leave here?"

She shrugged. "I'm a good typist. I'm good with Photoshop and the internet."

"Can you remember my name?"

"Sure. I'll probably see it again in the obituaries." A glimmer of a smile teased the corner of her lips. "Just kidding."

"Look me up. Then, send me an email. I'll help you find a job. My mom owns a bakery and wants to expand her business to online owners. I'm sure we can get you on at least part time until you find something better."

"Why do you want to help me? You didn't know I existed until ten minutes ago."

"You just feel like a kindred spirit." I stood and held out my hand as if we were two business people doing business. "I meant it, Lara. I'd like to help you."

She returned my shake. "I'll take you up on it. If you're still breathing."

I laughed. "Then my mom will help you. Do you like it here?"

"It's as great as a place like this can be. Ms. Marshall really does care about us girls, but she's a strict woman. She'll give you anything in her power, unless you step over the line. Then, she cracks down like a prison warden. She's exactly what us girls need."

I left feeling better than when I arrived. I'd made a new friend and possibly gained some insight into a disguise that would have me in the same place as Cherokee.

14

I stared in the mirror at my newly-dyed, ink black hair with fuschia tips and cried. The box said temporary hair color. I sure hoped so.

After raiding Cherokee's makeup drawer, I thought I had what I needed in order to look ten years younger. At least I hoped so. Maybe. If no one looked too closely.

I lined my eyes with a thick black eyeliner, then put on several coats of mascara. I put on a foundation, too light for my already pale skin, then stepped back from the mirror. I looked like a blue-eyed vampire.

Dressed all in black, with tight skinny jeans ripped at the knees, a too big sweatshirt that fell off one shoulder, showing the strap of a vibrant blue bra strap, and yellow flip-flops on my feet despite the chill in the air, I was as ready as I'd ever be. I slipped on the daisy ring and headed for the kitchen to wait for Mary Ann.

While I waited, I grabbed Dakota's dirtiest backpack from a hook next to the back door and dumped his school papers onto the table. If I was going to live in an abandoned warehouse, I intended to have a few comforts from home.

I shoved my Dad's old military green jacket inside along with a box of granola bars, some bottled water, bread, a jar of peanut butter and some cheese crackers. Food fit for a couple of homeless teens. I grabbed a couple of candles and some matches from a kitchen drawer.

There. A threadbare blanket and we were all set.

Mary Ann strolled in the back door, her blond hair dyed with blue streaks. She'd completely gone without makeup and looked about thirteen years old. She laughed. "You look like Morticia."

"Thanks. But am I young enough?"

"I think so." She plopped a pack on the table. "I've never run away before, so not really sure what to bring."

"We can always purchase a few odds and ends from a convenience store." I knocked on the basement door. "Mom will drop us off a couple of blocks from the warehouses."

"I'm coming!" Mom yelled up the basement stairs. "Oh." Her eyes practically bugged from her head when she entered the kitchen and got a look at us. "I hardly recognize my own daughter."

"What about me?" Angela, devoid of makeup, wearing a skirt of her daughter's, fur-lined boots, and a crocheted poncho, stepped into the room. "I'm going with you."

I wanted to object, but in her shoes, err, boots, I'd want the same thing. My sister was very pretty without the thick makeup. "With those, uh, your…chest, it's hard to imagine you as a teenager."

She rolled her eyes. "Don't be ridiculous. I taped them down."

Wayne barged through the back door, took one look at the three of us, and backed out, calling, "I'll come back when you're gone."

"What was that all about?" I asked, hefting my pack over my shoulder.

"He doesn't want to interfere with our leaving or to know too much about our disguises," Angela said. "He can't tell anyone what he doesn't know."

Smart. "Ready?" My heart pounded like a rock band.

Angela and Mary Ann nodded and moved past me to the front door. I took a deep breath and started to follow, stopping when Mom put a hand on my arm.

She kissed my cheek, blinking rapidly. "Be careful. Take care of those girls and bring back my granddaughter."

"I will." And my Matt.

Although I couldn't tell by the weight of the pack on my back, but knowing my Glock was there, along with my Tazer, made me feel a bit better. That, and the hour I'd spent in prayer the night before. God made me headstrong and slightly brave. I didn't think it came as a surprise to Him that I was venturing into the dark underbelly of my world to find those I loved. And, it didn't come as a surprise to me that He promised to be with me while I stormed the so-called castle. We would make a good team.

I'd expected Dakota to at least say goodbye to us, and glanced at his bedroom window. It was probably for the best. He didn't need to know our disguises, and we definitely wouldn't let him come along. Tossing my pack in the back with the other two, I climbed into the backseat with Mary Ann.

We made the forty minute drive in silence. Mom stopped the van in the alley behind an adult bookstore and a liquor store in the poor suburb of Blossom. A pretty name for a town that needed to be bulldozed down. Still, it was famous for its drugs and prostitution. It held our best chance for being abducted.

"I'll pray," Mom said. "Hard and without ceasing."

"Thank you." I retrieved my pack and stepped back from the vehicle. As the other two did the same, Mom drove away, leaving me feeling every bit the lost little girl I was pretending to be.

Tears stung my eyes and clogged my throat. I coughed. "Let's find a place to call home."

Amidst catcalls and whistles, we trudged down what might have been a lovely small town Main Street. Now, most of the buildings sported boarded up windows. In the distance rose a row of warehouses.

"Should we head there or find an unlocked store here?" I asked.

"Well, you said the party was in those warehouses. I say we go there. I bet there are still cots left behind." Mary Ann shuddered. "But, I don't think I can sleep on one. Not knowing that a young, frightened girl had sat there."

"We also need to be seen around here," Angela pointed out. "Someone will be bound to tell someone with power that three new girls have arrived."

She pulled a pill bottle from under her poncho and tossed a white capsule in her mouth. "What? We're druggies. Might as well play the part. These are left over from Mom's back injury two years ago. They might not be very potent, but if someone looks hard enough, they'll find a bottle of pain killers with someone else's name on them. And, that man over there is keeping a close watch on us. I'm just playing the part. You want one?"

I shook my head, hiding behind my mane of dyed tresses. Shy runaway I could do. Druggie might be a bit harder.

Mary Ann pretended to pop a pill and laughed shrilly, cocking her head toward the man watching. "Twenty bucks!"

He waved us off and stepped into the convenience store on the corner. I wasn't sure whether she was giving him the price of a bill or a moment of her time. Still, my face flushed and I increased my pace toward the warehouses looming ahead and left the other two to catch up.

It didn't take long before Angela and Mary Ann started bickering like the kids they were trying to imitate.

"I only brought one blanket, Angela. You should have thought about your own."

"My name is Lilly."

"Whatever."

Good point, though. "I'm Dusty."

Mary Ann sighed. "Fine. I've always wanted to be a Brittany. Still, I'm not giving *Lilly* my blanket tonight."

"She can have mine," I said. "I brought Dad's jacket."

"I want the jacket!" Angela jogged to my side.

"No. I brought it, I get to use it." Besides, it would bring me some much needed comfort.

"You have got to be the meanest person in Arkansas."

I whirled like a bear whose cub had just been threatened. "Excuse me?"

She took a step back.

"Am I not risking my life for your child? Do I not let you live in my house rent free? I ought to punch you in the throat!" I stomped away, letting the tears of fear and frustration fall.

By the time we reached the warehouses, the sun hung high and heavy in the sky, showering us with unusual warmth for that time of the year. And still, Angela and Mary Ann bickered.

Just as Wayne had left it, the warehouse where Bomberg had held his party was unlocked. I shoved against the heavy back door. It opened with a loud screech. I entered and stared at the last spot I'd seen Matt.

When Mary Ann started to step into the room across from me, I stopped her. "That's where the girl that I think was Cherokee was. Instead of picking a room, I think we should all stay together and bunk in the hall close to the bathroom."

"Good idea." Mary Ann pulled a blanket from her pack and spread it on the floor.

"Around the corner," I said.

"Right." She picked up the blanket and headed in the direction I'd pointed.

I touched the wall where Matt had leaned, then followed my friend. We'd find him, God and I, and Matt and Cherokee would be alive and well. I had to keep reminding myself of that. If I forgot, I wouldn't be able to go on.

The cheap cell phone I'd purchased so no one could track us, buzzed in my pocket. I dug it out. "Yeah?"

"Tell those two to stop arguing," Wayne said. "Your nephew and I don't want to listen to hours of drama."

"Dakota is with you?"

"Yes. He's in charge of video surveillance."

I closed my eyes in relief. "Well, teenage girls have drama, don't they?"

"Just tell them to stop." Click.

I swiped the back of my hand across my face to dry it. "Wayne said stop fighting."

"He can see us?" Angela stared at the walls and the ceiling. "Are there cameras?"

Mary Ann gave an evil grin. "I have one in my necklace and Stormi has one in her ring. I guess the spy equipment ran out before you could get one."

I sighed and spread out my blanket on the floor. It was going to be a long couple of days. "We need a plan. Let's come up with one."

Finished squabbling, they sat cross-legged on Mary Ann's blanket and stared at me like eager students. "I said we need a plan. Not I need a plan. I can't do this alone."

"Just lead us," Mary Ann said.

Angela nodded.

"This place is fine for night, but what do we do during the day? Wander the streets aimlessly?"

Mary Ann raised her hand. "I think one of us should try robbing a store, then racing away before getting caught. It would help our disguise."

"Or," Angela straightened, "we could actually try selling ourselves."

"What happens if someone takes us up on it?" Mary Ann glanced at her as if she'd sprouted antennas. "I'm not doing that."

"Me either." Angela managed to look shocked. "I have a powder that helps you sleep. We could pour it in—"

"Enough." Where did she get these things? A few months ago, she'd flirted with a suspect and slipped him something to put him to sleep so she wouldn't have to follow through with her flirtation. I was afraid my sister had an illegal side to her.

I thought my hardest, trying to come up with a better plan than they'd come up with. All I had was the idea of us wandering the streets. Did runaways do that? Or did they prefer to stay hidden? Except hiding wouldn't accomplish our goal of getting snatched.

I wrapped my arms around my bent knees and rested my chin on them. "At dusk, we'll go to the convenience store and buy sodas. We'll try to look as suspicious as possible. If we're seen enough, doing nothing but loitering, someone is bound to say something to someone."

"They might call the cops," Angela pointed out.

"Then Wayne will have to play defense for us." I didn't have another plan. I really was lost.

15

I leaped from my hard bed on the concrete floor when the sound of shuffling feet woke me. I nudged the other two women with my foot.

"What?" Angela shouted, scooting against the wall. Not a lot of bravery there.

"Hush." I frowned. Seriously. I sometimes wondered what went through my sister's head.

"There's an old woman looking for a storm," a drunk man sang as he staggered past us. "She's pacing outside waiting to see." He focused clear eyes on me, winked, and continued on his way.

"Stay here," I hissed at Angela and Mary Ann. "If I'm not back in fifteen minutes, hunt that drunk down." I whirled and sprinted from the building and around the corner.

I stood on the sidewalk and bent over to catch my breath. Eventually, running would get easier, right?

A bag lady pushed a shiny shopping cart piled high with bags past me, turned at the intersection, and came back in my direction. White teeth flashed in a dirty face.

"Mom?" I peered through the dark.

She gave an almost imperceptible shake of her head. "I might have something that interests you, sweetie." Mom slash bag lady pulled a brown paper sack from her cart. "But it will cost you." She mouthed, "We're being watched."

"I don't have a lot of money." I fought the strong urge to turn and see who was watching. "Is five dollars enough?" I fished the bill from my pocket and handed it to her.

"It's more than I have now. Nice doing business with you." She strolled away, leaving my heart lodged in my throat at the danger she put herself in by coming to where I was.

I clutched the paper sack until she was out of sight, then turned. The form of a man ducked around the building. With one more glance in the direction Mom had gone, I hurried back to the others.

"You bought booze?" Angela made a move for the bag the moment I returned.

"Hush." Why did I have to use that word so much in regards to my sister? I peered into the bag. An amber colored bottle with a few drops of beer, from the smell of it, nestled inside. A small water-proof tube stuck from the neck of the bottle. Inside the tube was a rolled up piece of paper.

I pulled out the paper and handed the bottle to Angela, who upended it almost immediately. I shuddered. "You don't know where that came from."

"Do you?" she shrugged.

I lowered my voice. "Mom gave it to me."

"So, everything is good."

"But, you didn't know that."

"I'm stressed right now." Her eyes welled with tears. "Have some compassion."

It wasn't my place to straighten out my sister. Mom had tried for years. Angela was…Angela, with all her quirks and questionable morals. I'd let God handle her. He was way more capable.

"What does the note say?" Mary Ann crawled closer. "Who is it from?"

"It's from Mom," I whispered. The other two read over my shoulder.

Girls,

There's been a development. Don't trust anyone. I mean it. Someone close to us is not who he seems. The young man has found out some disturbing information and gone into hiding. Don't be alarmed. I will care for him.

The bag lady

"Give me your lighter." I held out my hand to Angela.

"How do you know I have one?"

"I know you still carry one even if you did quit smoking."

She sighed and dug around in her pack, finally emerging with it.

I burned the note, letting the ashes fall

to the floor. I knew who the young man was. It had to be Dakota. Possibly Rusty, but I was going with my nephew. As for the someone close we couldn't trust, I prayed with all my heart she didn't mean Wayne. I pulled the spy ring from my finger, turned the little knob that switched it off, and dropped it in my pocket.

Mary Ann watched me and removed her necklace. "We really are on our own."

"I'm afraid so."

I ignored the buzzing of my cell phone. It didn't take a genius to know Wayne was trying to call.

Several minutes later, the drunk returned. He slid down the wall a few feet from us and exhaled sharply. Without saying a word, he crossed his arms and went to sleep. Or at least pretended to. The more I thought about it, the more I figured he wasn't drunk, but undercover. I smiled and rolled up in my blanket, feeling safer than I had since leaving home.

When I woke a few hours later, the man was gone. I stretched, feeling every bit of my twenty-eight years. Empty cracker wrappers told me the other two had eaten. Their voices drifted from the direction of the bathroom. I got painfully to my feet and went to join them.

"What now?" Mary Ann asked as she applied a small amount of makeup in the speckled mirror. "Want to make an appearance at the convenience store? Is that where runaways might hang out?"

"I'll go stand on the street corner," Angela said from her seat on the closed toilet. "Maybe I can coerce some fool into saying something."

If anyone could, it was my shapely sister. I still didn't think anyone would believe her to be nineteen, but once she started promising them things, they probably wouldn't care. The lack of heavy makeup helped her look younger. Maybe we'd be okay.

"I'll stand outside and keep watch while you two do your thing. Someone has to be able to cry the alarm if something goes wrong."

After we'd cleaned up the best we could in a tiny bathroom sink, we headed into a cloudy mid-morning. A gray sky promised rain. Wonderful. Our new home would be cold and damp. We walked the thirty minutes to "downtown".

Angela took off her poncho, revealing a low-cut blouse. She tugged her skirt higher and leaned against a lamp pole, propping one foot behind her as if she'd been soliciting her entire life. Maybe she had, in a way. Her looks had gotten her through school, barely, and she rarely went unemployed for long after losing a job. Me? I had to work for everything I had.

I took my station against the dirty wall of the adult bookstore and watched as Mary Ann practically skipped into the convenience store. I knew she was worried about her brother, but her teenage acting ought to earn her an academy award. Of the three of us, she was the most believable.

A bag lady shuffled down the opposite side of the street. I almost ran over, but realized the poor thing limped from a club foot. Even Mom couldn't pull that off. Our drunk friend lounged in the doorway of an empty storefront. I hoped that someday I'd have a chance to thank him for looking out for us.

A trio of African American young men laughed and shoved each other past us, doing a double take when they caught a glimpse of Angela. One of them made a ribald comment. His friends laughed.

"You should be in school," Angela said. "Now, unless you got money, get out of here."

Another few choice words left their mouths before they followed her advice. I smiled. Why did I worry about her? She was a champ at survival.

Several cars pulled up alongside her. Angela leaned in, talked for a bit, and waved them on their way.

After what seemed like an eternity, Mary Ann bounded from the convenience store with a bag of potato chips and a liter of soda. If the bulge under her shirt was any indication, she'd managed to follow through with her shoplifting idea.

"Let's go. Quickly," she sang, glancing over her shoulder. "The clerk will get suspicious soon enough."

Waving for Angela to follow, we

headed back to the warehouse as the first raindrops started to fall. Inside, I pulled the door closed and felt along the wall until reaching our meager pile of belongings. I located the candle, melted the bottom a bit, and stuck it to the floor before lighting the wick. Home sweet home.

"Spill it, girls. What did you find out?" I glanced from one to the other, the worry in their eyes more pronounced in the flickering light of the candle.

"The store clerk warned me no less than five times that young girls in this part of town have a way of disappearing. He suggested a halfway house about two blocks from here, but said they only have a sliver of a chance of staying there before a girl disappears." She shook her head. "How have we not heard of this on the news?"

"These are throw-away kids," Angela said. "Runaways, foster kids, homeless. Either there isn't anyone to care, or not enough funds to go looking. That's why it's important we stop this here. At least in our corner of the world."

I agreed. Hopefully, stopping it meant bringing our loved ones home safe.

"One of the guys who pulled up in front of me was a cop," she said. "I pointed him toward Wayne and asked him to move along. The other one didn't have the funds to purchase anything, and acting or not, it isn't free. I learned nothing. Is your cell phone buzzing?"

"Yes." I cupped my hand over my hip pocket. "Our warning note said not to trust anyone. You read it. So, I'm following the advice."

"Sometimes you have to take chances." Our guard, or angel, or drunken vagrant, whatever he was, spoke from a dark corner of the hall. "Three girls alone against these people…not a good idea."

"We'll take that into consideration. Thank you." I turned my back on him. Not trusting anyone, meant him, too, even if I did feel safer with him around. I opened my pack, made sure my gun and Tazer were within easy reach, and pulled out a bottle of water.

The crackle of the potato chip bag seemed abnormally loud in the concrete corridor. Anyone looking for three easy victims, wouldn't have a hard time finding us. Why hadn't we been taken?

I twisted off the top of the bottle and took a big gulp as Mary Ann lifted her shirt, revealing a teen throb magazine, a tube of lipstick, and a bottle of bumble gum pink fingernail polish. "I figured this is what a teen would steal," she said. "I'll pay for them when this is all over. If I'm able to."

Angela lifted her arm and sniffed her arm pit. "I need a shower."

"We all do. Let's check out the other hallway." I got to my feet. "It's the one I wasn't allowed to go in at the party. Maybe there's a shower in there."

"I wouldn't," our guardian said. "You might see something you won't like."

"That's the point of us being here," I snapped. "To put a stop to things we don't like."

Leaving the others to follow, I marched to the large room where the party had been held. Had it really only been a couple of days?

I stepped into the cavernous room.

Our footsteps echoed in the emptiness. The doorway across from us loomed like the mouth of a foul beast. My heart rate increased. Maybe the vagrant was right. Maybe it wasn't a good idea. Maybe it was a trap!

I took a step back.

Angela shoved against me. "Don't be a scaredy-cat."

"Then you go first."

"Nope. It's your idea."

"Mary Ann, I mean, Brittany?"

"Not a chance."

"For crying out loud." Our drunken friend whipped off his stringy wing and hat, revealing the boyishly handsome face of Mary Ann's boyfriend, Officer Michael Barker.

"You three are the hardest assignment I've ever had."

16

Mary Ann squealed and threw her arms around Michael's neck. I groaned. If anyone was watching, our cover was officially blown.

"Now what?" I crossed my arms and glared. "No one is going to believe a silicone boobed teen girl, another with the beginnings of crow's feet, and now a man? The only one who might have pulled off this charade was Mary Ann. We have no chance now."

"It never worked." Michael peeled Mary Ann's arms off him. "That's why I'm here. You turned off the recording device so Wayne wasn't able to fill you in. Your mother heard something from Dakota, you heard from—"

"Just tell us what it is."

"Those responsible for the slavery ring are after you, and only you. Your sister and Mary Ann are collateral damage."

"Why? It isn't like I fit the mold of what they want."

His face grew serious. "Because you have a reputation for finding out what you want to know. They're running scared. That's why I'm here and leaving the police department very short-handed."

"Then, I suppose we should solve this immediately." The last thing I wanted was my sister and best friend tossed aside like yesterday's garbage, just so some freak could get to me. Who knew writing true mystery romances could be so dangerous? Since that first book, I'd encountered one murderer after another. Maybe I should switch to romantic comedy.

I tossed my hair and took a step into the hall of doom. Dramatic, but I seriously doubted we would discover anything warm and fuzzy there. While the other hall was dark and damp, this corridor was oppressive. As if something heavy weighed upon the air. It wasn't too far of a stretch to believe the feeling was in my mind. Still, I found it hard to breathe.

Not wanting the others to know of my rising anxiety level, I marched forward. Room and cell-like room held only a cot. Doors, with small windows with sliding panels, hung open. My stomach churned. I'd served dessert while atrocities against young girls went on mere yards away. Had it really only been two days?

If those responsible saw through our ruse, there was nothing left to do but go home. "Let's pack up and make a new plan."

Angela planted herself in my path. "My baby is out there."

"And we need a plan to get her back." I met Michael's gaze. "How can I get a message to these people letting them know I'm ready to meet?"

"Let's discuss it with Wayne."

"Can we trust him?"

Angela snorted. "Now you're being ridiculous." She shoved past me. "Let's go."

"You two make enough noise to wake the dead." Dakota stepped around the corner, grinning.

Angela screamed and wrapped him in her arms. "What are you doing here?"

"I figured this is where y'all were hiding, so I came to join you."

My shoulders slumped. "I'll stay here with him. The rest of you go home and make sure we live long enough to find Matt and Cherokee." If he couldn't go home, he definitely couldn't stay out there alone.

"Can't we pretend he's missing?" Mary Ann asked. "We would have keep him in the house." She glanced around the warehouse. "It was hard enough with us three, staying here, but seeing these rooms…I shudder to think of the two of you alone here. Evil resides in these walls."

"You're right. Let's all go home." Already a plan was formulating in my mind. A plan that would put me in the most danger I'd ever been in, but one that would, hopefully, protect the family left behind.

After gathering our belongings, we waited in the doorway for an hour until

Mom arrived with the van. Her sparkling grin cut through the gloom of the day like a lighthouse beacon. She might be worried about her granddaughter, but having her own daughters back under her roof would ease the worry a bit.

The ride home was silent, cut only by the thwump of the windshield wipers and the rain pounding on the hood. "We were idiots," I said. "How could we have actually thought masquerading as teenage girls was a good idea?"

"It would have worked," Michael said, "if those responsible hadn't been alerted."

"That's why I wrote the note." Mom inhaled sharply through her nose. "I suspect we have a mole. But, I'm not ready to spill my suspicions just yet."

"The department could make you," Michael pointed out.

"They could try." She shrugged. "Unless you taped this conversation without my permission, it's your word against mine. And if you did tape us, it would never hold up in court."

"You could be impeding an

investigation."

"Then, arrest me." She whipped the steering wheel taking us sharply around the curve.

I grabbed the handle to the right of my head. The poor rookie would figure out soon enough not to rile my mother. When she got something stuck in her craw, so to speak, she was like a snapping turtle latched on until the thunder rolled. I was always blessed to have her on my side.

Mom pulled as close to the house as possible, but we were still all soaked by the time we got in the house. "Upstairs." She pointed at Dakota. "You aren't here. You've run away. Remember that."

"Yes, ma'am." He took the stairs two at a time. Within seconds, loud music radiated from his room. Very subtle that young man.

"Why did you turn off your ring?" Wayne crossed his massive arms. "It was a foolish, foolhardy move that required me removing Officer Barker from his job. Without Detective Steele here, we cannot afford to move anymore manpower."

"I'll write him a check. That should make it worth his time." I headed for the kitchen and some coffee.

"Don't be flippant with me." He followed.

I whirled, coffee pot in one hand, and poked him in the chest with my finger. "Then don't pull that macho act with me! My nerves are strung so tight, you could have a guitar solo with them." I swallowed back tears. "I'm tired, I'm hungry, I'm worried and scared, not to mention my hair is black. Black!" I thrust the coffee pot under the faucet and slapped the water on.

Without saying another word, Wayne took the pot from me. He motioned his head toward the upstairs.

I nodded. A shower and bed sounded exactly like what I needed. If sleep eluded me, I'd return for the coffee.

As I stood in the shower, I stared at the drain trying to see whether the dye was washing out. Something dark swirled at my feet. It wasn't until I got out and glanced in the mirror that I realized it had been my eye liner. Matt would get a laugh out of the hair dye refusing to fade. I prayed that he would get that chance.

Were they mistreating him? Had they drugged Cherokee and forced her to do unspeakable things? Could I dare hope that the two of them were merely locked up until things died down? Did my niece know that Matt was close by? Was he?

Despite the questions cycling through my mind like a tornado, I fell asleep almost instantly. When I woke, the house was quiet. The clock said four a.m. I'd slept the day and most of the night.

I climbed out of bed and headed to the kitchen where Wayne sat hunkered over a laptop at the kitchen table. "I kept the pot hot," he said. He leaned back in his chair and ran his hands over his face. "I've been trying to find everything I can on Carol Forbes. Until she became a foster parent, it was like she didn't exist."

"Could the state have missed that?" I breathed deep of the java pouring into my cup. "I mean, don't you have to have fingerprints done and references? Things like that?"

"Yeah, but someone didn't pay

attention to the lack of a birth certificate. Not that it isn't as easy to falsify, and other records." He shook his head. "Maybe I'm just too tired to make sense of it."

I held the mug out to him.

"No, thanks. I've had enough to give me a heart attack."

"Go get some sleep. I'll see if I can find anything."

"Time is running out." He glanced at me with red-rimmed eyes. "My partner is depending on me. I don't have time to sleep."

"You won't be a lot of good to us if you don't." I decided at that moment that whoever Mom meant we couldn't trust, it wasn't Wayne. "You're doing all you can. Get at least a two-hour nap."

He nodded. "Wake me at six-thirty." He headed for the living room.

I had no intention of waking him. The man needed sleep.

I turned his laptop to where I could see the screen. Carol Forbes's face stared back at me from a driver's license photo. Who are you really, Carol? What would cause you to sell young girls?

The screen went to sleep and, since I didn't know Wayne's password, there wasn't much more I could do. I grabbed my trusty fluorescent pink clipboard from next to the refrigerator and pulled a pencil from the cup next to the phone. Maybe some old-fashioned note taking would clear my head.

"You're up early," Mom said as she appeared at the top of the basement stairs.

"Or late, if you consider how long I slept." I studied her for a minute, taking in the bags under her eyes, and the lines in her usually smooth skin. "Who do you suspect, Mom?"

"I can't tell you. If I'm wrong, and focus is put on this person when it should be put elsewhere, I'll never forgive myself. If, when, I have enough information, you'll be the first to know."

"Are you putting yourself in danger?"

"Are you?"

"Touche."

She poured a cup of coffee and joined me at the table. "What are you thinking?"

"I'm thinking I want to go back to

Carol's house. There has to be something left behind. Something we missed." Since we'd almost been discovered by a potential murderer, it was quite possible.

"When do you want to go? It'll be light soon." She glanced at the window where sunlight was beginning to peek through the curtains.

"Maybe going during the light of day will be less suspicious. We are the Neighborhood Watch. We could go on the pretense of checking the yard and making sure vandals haven't disturbed the house. I don't have any other ideas. Time is flying by and I'm so worried about Matt and Cherokee, that I feel ill. If we don't discover something at the house, then I'll keep pounding the pavements."

She raised her mug in a toast. "Here's to a wonderful idea! Let's not forget our guns."

"Our guns?" I widened my eyes.

She raised her chin. "I bought one. It has a purple handle. Or is it called a grip? Anyway, I love it."

I groaned. The world would never be the same.

17

Wearing normal jogging attire, mine black and hot pink, Mom's highlighter yellow and black, we jogged down the sidewalk toward Carol's former home. Jogged being a very relative term. It was always obvious we weren't trying to be secretive. Not with Mom waving and "yoo-hooing" to everyone we passed, or with Sadie wanting to squat every three feet.

It took thirty minutes to make our way to the house which sat two blocks away. If we'd been moving any slower, we would have been going backward.

"What are you two up to this morning?" Betty Rogers, a crotchety neighbor who passed around an unsuccessful petition a few months ago to have me run out of the neighborhood, stepped from around an untrimmed evergreen bush. After being held prisoner with me and Mom, we'd formed a shaky alliance. Still, she kept looking over her shoulder toward her house in an uncharacteristically nervous fashion, which set my senses tingling.

"Uh, we're out for a jog." I followed her gaze. The front curtains twitched.

"Very good. Wonderful." She beckoned with one finger for us to step closer.

Mom and I glanced at each other and stepped behind the bush.

"I have a girl in my house," Betty whispered, frowning at the sight of our guns sticking up from the waist of our pants. Or mine, anyway. Mom's was hidden in a fanny pack. "I need you to remove her. I'm not made out for a life of danger. I'm too old."

"Is she a family member?" I asked.

"No. Never met her before the other day. I found her hiding in my shed."

"Have you called the police?"

She sniffed. "They aren't exactly keen on responding to me after all the times I called on you. It seems you're an officer's pet."

"I don't mean to be disrespectful, Mrs. Rogers," I said, "but Mom and I are on a mission—"

"I know what you're doing. I get around." She crossed her arms. "This is one of those girls. The heavy one."

"Are you sure?"

"I told you I get around. I know what goes on. Are you going to help or not?"

"I am."

Mom and I followed her across her lawn and around to the back of the house. Mrs. Rogers shook her head and pointed to Sadie. "She stays outside. I don't want the hair or the drool."

My dog didn't drool. "Sorry, girl." I looped her leash around a post on her back patio and entered into a kitchen so stark white, I was momentarily blinded. The only spot of color, if a person was to consider black a color, was the girl dressed all in black. Until Mom and I, with our colorful vibrancy, entered, the room was a cold place indeed.

"I told you not to tell anyone!" Miranda Jones stomped her foot, no longer a chubby teen, she'd lost at least twenty pounds. A temporary thing from the looks of a half-eaten plate of cookies on the table.

"I can't keep you."

"But they're after her." She pointed at me.

"Can you tell me who they are?" As a person might approach a skittish horse, I took slow steps toward her, my hand outstretched. "If I know, maybe I can stop this."

"No one can stop this." She plopped into a chair. "They're going to kill you, and me, and probably your mom, too."

"Then help us. We're going to the house. Do you know of any place Carol might have hid important information?"

"She'd be stupid to keep stuff like that around, but I do know of a hidden panel in the wall." Miranda twisted her mouth as she thought. "You promise to get me somewhere safe?"

"I promise." I'd turn her over to Wayne for safekeeping the moment we were finished searching. "They have my niece and my boyfriend."

"Then you need to pray for their safety." She snagged two cookies and headed for the back door.

"Maybe you should tell us where the panel is. We can take you somewhere safe first."

The terror in her eyes as she glanced over her shoulder confirmed I'd made the right decision. "The walls have that old paneling. The type in the old movies from the 70s."

I nodded.

"As you're going down the hall, count each panel. When you reach twenty-three, you can slide it free."

Next to a wall phone, who had those anymore? was a pad of paper and a jar of pencils. I snagged one and wrote a quick note explaining what was happening, then handed it to Betty. "Take this to my house. Officer Wayne Jones is there. Give him this note. He'll make sure Miranda is safe."

Betty nodded. "Come on, girl. We're taking a hike through the woods. This is probably the only time I'm glad that tick-infested stand of trees borders this community."

I gave Miranda a quick hug. "It will be okay."

She nodded. "Talk to the old man who owns the car repair place. He knows things." With those parting words, she raced out the door and into the trees.

"Don't let me die being a good Samaritan," Betty said before following Miranda.

I didn't intend on anyone dying. After retrieving Sadie, who napped under a Magnolia tree, Mom and I resumed our pretense of jogging to Carol's house.

Crime scene tape, faded by the autumn sun, had lost its grip on one stake in the ground and waved an eerie greeting as a breeze lifted it. As we stepped onto the driveway, a cloud slid in front of the sun. I shuddered and reached for Mom's hand.

"We'll be fine. It will all be fine." She closed her eyes, said a silent prayer, and squeezed my hand before releasing it. "Let's go move that panel."

"Right." Showing more bravery than I felt, I headed for the back door, hoping it was unlocked like last time. It wasn't.

Mom picked up a rock from a nearby flowerbed border and shattered the window on the door. With a shrug, she reached in and flipped the latch. "We're already breaking the law, again, so why not go all the way?"

I released Sadie's leash and let her follow us inside. Maybe she could give a warning if someone came. Not likely, considering she was less brave than me, but miracles could happen.

The house didn't seem near as frightening as it had the last time. Without the cover of darkness, it looked like any other house built and decorated in the 1970s. Plain cabinets, gold countertops, wood paneling, and green shag carpet. No wonder the poor house was still a rental. It would take a small fortune to renovate it, and houses in Oak Meadows weren't cheap.

Since there most likely wouldn't be anything left that wasn't hidden, I made a beeline for the hallway and started counting.

"If there is something important here,

or was here, why would it be left behind?"

"That's probably what the intruder was looking for when we were here last time." I backed up to start counting again. "We scared him off." But…he had had a box with him. I couldn't help but wonder what he'd gotten away with.

"Good point."

I got to eleven.

Mom leaned against the wall. "How do you think Miranda got away? Do you think she saw Cherokee?"

"We'll ask her when we get back to the house. Please let me count." I started over. Again.

This time I made it to twenty and stared at the infamous panel. I felt around the edges until my fingernail slipped into a slot. I popped off the panel. A manila envelope was propped between the two by fours. I grabbed it, slid it under my shirt, and replaced the piece of paneling. "Let's go."

Mom had her gun out. "We're being watched. There. By the tree." She motioned out a bedroom window. "Someone knows we're here." Her eyes narrowed. "Someone whose shape looks very familiar."

Great. Wonderful. We'd probably found the evidence we needed, but would be killed before using it. "Out the back. Fast and quiet." Feeling like a heroine from an action spy thriller, I pulled my own weapon and led the way. *Please, God, don't let me have to shoot someone.*

The moment we stepped outside, we raced for the next yard and slipped through an unlocked gate. This side of the community didn't have the trees ours did. Instead, we'd have to use the protection of houses. I hoped the person watching wouldn't notice we were gone for a few more minutes. At least until we were back on the street where any of the neighbors could see us.

Pounding footsteps alerted us to the fact we were being followed. I plastered my back against the wall of a house and held my weapon at the ready. Remembering what Matt had told me, I kept my finger to the side of the gun so I wouldn't pull it too quickly.

A man careened around the corner.

Mom screamed.

Her gun fired.

Rusty shrieked.

My knees sagged. "We could have killed you, Rusty."

"Bad man coming. Follow me." He squeezed through a hedge.

Without a second thought, I shoved Mom ahead and followed. We were in Rusty's backyard. Ducking through fences or hedges, anywhere there was an opening, he led us through until my hair was tangled, my pants ripped, and I realized I'd left Sadie behind.

"Sadie." I forced her name from my tortured throat.

"She ran home." Rusty held a finger to his lips. "Dog safe. You're not."

I nodded. He hadn't made this much sense in the months I'd known him.

He waved us on again. When we crossed onto the street where I lived, we came out of hiding and tried to appear as casual as possible as we walked down the sidewalk.

"Mom. Back at the house you said the person out the window looked familiar.

Who was it?"

She opened her mouth to answer.

A shot rang out.

Mom collapsed to the ground as a pool of blood spread under her head.

Rusty screamed, or maybe it was me, since the big man scooped my mother into his arms as if she weighed nothing and ran for my house. Another shot rang out. He stumbled, but kept running.

I put my finger on the trigger and glanced back.

The shooter hid in the shadows of a willow tree. His next shot rang out as we ducked behind Mom's trusty van. By now, Wayne was outside, his weapon drawn, and crouched beside us.

"Who is it?"

I shook my head. "Mom thought she knew, but…"

He took one look at her and grabbed his cell phone out of his pocket.

Rusty cradled Mom in his arms. Big crocodile tears ran down his cheeks as he rocked back and forth.

Dread filled me to my core.

18

"Is she dead?" I crawled toward her, my vision obscured by my tears.

Wayne pulled me back behind the protection of the van. "Let me check." Sirens wailed in the distance as he moved to my mother. Our attacker's shots ceased. Wayne put his fingers against Mom's pulse. "She's alive. It looks like the bullet grazed her, but she has a knot on her forehead the size of a golf ball."

He peered over the van's hood as the first of the emergency personnel arrived. Several police officers did a quick sweep of the area. "They're waving that the shooter's gone," Wayne said. "We can get up now."

The moment the ambulance came to a screeching halt in front of the house,

Angela burst through the front door and ran, wailing, toward us. "Mama!"

Wayne stepped in front of her and wrapped his arms around her. "She's alive. There's no need to work yourself into a frenzy."

The man knew my sister well. I wiped the tears from my face and hovered as the paramedics assessed her situation, making a nuisance of myself until they asked me to step back. They placed Mom on a gurney and loaded her into the ambulance. I jumped in next to her and gave them a look that defied them to say anything against me riding along.

Wayne told Rusty to stay down, propped Angela against the van, and marched to meet the arriving Michael Barker. With Matt gone and Wayne busy with us, the poor town was seriously understaffed for emergencies. I squashed down the bit of guilt I felt about monopolizing the time of the local police officers and concentrated on my mother.

Blood matted hair the same shade as mine to her face. Always fair-skinned, the pallor of her skin caused me to check for myself that she still breathed. I leaned close, feeling the whisper of her breath on my cheek. I closed my eyes and sent a prayer of thanksgiving to God. I'd come so close to losing her. I still could, but as long as she drew breath, there was hope.

The ambulance made the drive to the hospital twenty miles away in fifteen minutes. I hopped down without waiting for help and jogged alongside the gurney as we raced into the Emergency Room.

I couldn't take my eyes off Mom's face, hoping, praying she'd open her eyes and say something snarky. A woman in mint green scrubs stopped me before I could follow Mom into an examining room. I sighed and turned to the waiting room as another gurney rolled up.

"Miss Stormi?" Rusty held out his hand.

"You were shot?" I ran my gaze over his body, noticing for the first time the hole in his upper leg as I took his hand.

"You have to come with me. Don't let them take me past those doors alone. People don't come back." His grip ground my fingers together.

I glanced at the doctor next to the gurney. The man shrugged, then motioned his head toward the examining room next to where they had taken Mom. I nodded. If I couldn't be with her, I'd be with the sweet man who had, quite possibly, saved her life.

The doctor let me stay only until Rusty succumbed to the effects of a shot to relax him. I patted his cheek, and blinked back tears as they wheeled him to surgery.

Instead of heading for the waiting room, I slipped down a different hall, then another, not sure where I was going, but feeling as if I needed to be there. Time was of the essence.

I ended up on the patient floor. I glanced at name plaques next to the doors until I saw the name Brian Colville. Could this be Dakota's friend? The young man I'd meant to visit several times, but had never gotten the chance?

I knocked and pushed open the door. Yes, it was the same young man who had lain bleeding on the street. Now, purple and yellow bruises mottled his skin. He was dressed to leave the hospital in jeans and a tee shirt sporting the logo of a rock band. "Brian, I'm Dakota's aunt."

He glanced around me. "I know who you are. You have to leave."

"I'd like to ask you a few questions."

"I'm going away for a while. My parents will be here soon. If those men find out—"

"What men, Brian?" I stepped around the curtain out of view of the door. "Please talk to me."

"They said if I told, then I'd get more than a beating the next time." He closed his eyes. "My parents just think it was some jerks that beat me up over my skateboard. I want them to think that. Those men threatened to hurt my parents if I said anything to the cops."

"I won't say anything to them, and I'm not a cop."

He opened his eyes and stared at me for a few minutes. "I don't know all of their names. One of them starts with a B. He's a real slimy character. The old man at the auto place knows him, I think. I've seen them talking together."

"Why are you involved?" I put a hand on his shoulder, feeling the frailty of his bones. "You haven't been eating or sleeping, have you?"

He shook his head. "I keep having nightmares. They're horrible. Rosie is my girl, but those men make her do things. When they found out we were seeing each other, they beat her, then came after me." His eyes shimmered with tears. "I don't care what she's done. I really, really like her, Miss Nelson."

"She's a very pretty girl. What else do you know?"

"That Carol woman works for them. Rosie told me a lot. She wanted me to help her get away. Carol takes in foster kids. Only teenage girls. You know why."

Unfortunately, I did, and the knowledge curdled my blood. "Do you know where they took the girls?"

"Do you know that old motel on the highway? The Pink Flamingo?"

"Yes. It's been closed for years."

"That's—" Men's voices reached us from the doorway. Brian's eyes bugged.

I grabbed the only weapon I could

find, the IV stand, having left my gun on the ground next to Mom's van. It was heavier than I thought. The moment a man stepped around the curtain, a man I'd seen guarding the hall of doom at the party, I swung the stand, smashing it into the side of his head. "Run, Brian!"

He leaped from the bed and raced for the nurse's station. I was close on his heels.

"Call the police!" I told the wide-eyed nurses as Brian and I ducked behind the counter.

A woman screamed.

"That's my mom." Brian started to stand.

I yanked him back down. "You aren't going anywhere until the police arrive."

"We have armed guards in the hospital," a nurse whispered. "It will only be a few minutes before they arrive."

It was less than two. I peered over the counter as the man I'd hit was dragged away in handcuffs. A cut above his left ear bled. Good. I wish I'd done more damage. I stood up and swayed until a nurse lowered me to a chair.

"You brave thing." She shoved a Styrofoam cup of water into my hands. "Would you like a doctor to check you over?"

"No. My mother is down the hall. I need to go to her."

"I'll have someone escort you." She waved over an orderly who didn't look much older than my nephew.

Brian was having his face covered with kisses from his mother. His father glared protectively at anyone who passed by. I wished them luck.

"Miss?" Mr. Colville called. "Thank you."

I gave a sad smile, so tired of the violence, and followed Doogie Howser number two to the elevator. He tried engaging me in general conversation, but I stared at the water in my cup and didn't answer. I now knew the possible location of Cherokee and Matt. Did I share the information with Wayne or go alone? I couldn't stand to have anyone else harmed.

Wayne and Angela greeted me in the hall where I'd left Mom. "They've moved her to a room," Wayne said. "She has a concussion. They have her heavily medicated to keep her asleep until the swelling in her head goes down."

I wanted to cry. Instead, I squared my shoulders. "I have some things to tell you. But, not here. First, we wait until Rusty gets out of surgery."

We waited two hours before a doctor came to get us. "Mr. Hensen made it out of surgery just fine," he said. "We'll keep him for a few days, then he'll be released with crutches. Will there be someone available during his recovery?"

"I will." I'd take the man home and treat him better than he'd ever been treated. Mom would too, once she woke up. Rusty would be the brother I'd never had.

I turned to Wayne and Angela. "Let's go home. We have a plan of attack to formulate."

19

"You hit someone over the head at the hospital?" Wayne's eyes were the size of silver dollars.

"For the third time…yes." I'd do anything to get closer to rescuing Matt. Every minute, every second, put the chances of bringing him home safe at risk. If it meant cold-cocking someone, I'd do it again. "I'm pretty sure he would have killed Brian."

"You're the bravest person I know," Mary Ann said. She'd heard the gunshots and rushed to the house as the ambulance pulled out of our driveway. Wayne had explained to her what had happened and she'd agreed to stay with Dakota.

"Not so much. It was more instinct, really."

"The kid said the Pink Flamingo is where the girls are?" Wayne cocked his head, tapping an ink pen on the pad of paper in front of him.

"Why are you questioning me for the third time on everything?" I crossed my arms and glared. "We need to take action."

"I'm alerting the authorities as we speak." He reached for his phone on the table in front of him.

I put my hand over his to stop him. "We should check it out first. I know it's protocol to call in reinforcements, but if we're so close…right on the edge of getting Cherokee and Matt back…I want to make sure they're actually there so we didn't risk tipping off the bad guys. Is that something we can do without getting into too much trouble?"

"I'll head over there and investigate."

"I'll go with you. All I need to do is put on my stupid disguise, that will only work from far away. But…" I grinned, "I don't want anyone to get close."

"I suppose if someone questions us, I purchased you for the hour."

My grin faded. What a way to bring it all back into focus. We weren't playing pretend. Lives hung in the balance. My gaze clashed with his. We could very well die that day.

I had a tendency to, even when under extreme stress such as I had been the last few days, to push things to the back of my mind when feeling overwhelmed. I'd sort through it when life gave me a breather. I could pretend it wasn't as bad as it seemed. The bad part of that was when someone yanked it back to the forefront, it was like getting hit with a tsunami.

Maybe it was a mental illness. Maybe I needed to have my head checked when this was all over. If I still had a head.

"Mom said the person who shot at us looked familiar. Before she could say more, she was…"

"We'll find him." A muscle ticked in Wayne's jaw.

"Did someone get my gun off the lawn?" I asked.

"I did." Mary Ann opened a kitchen drawer and handed it to me. "I'll stay here with Dakota and call you with regular updates on your mom and Rusty."

Tears pricked my eyes. "Thank you." I glanced at Angela, who sat, shoulders slumped, face in hands, at the table. I sent Mary Ann a quiet request to look after my sister as I slipped my gun into the backpack on the table.

She nodded, her face grim. "As if they were my own. Michael will be here as often as he is able. We'll pray without ceasing."

"Do you know Mr. Clean?" Suddenly remembering our guardian angel from the party, I whirled to face Wayne.

"Who?" His brow furrowed.

I explained. "Undercover?"

"Most likely." A spark of hope leaped into his eyes. "This is the best news we've had in what seems like a long time. Matt isn't in there alone."

"Cherokee?" Angela looked up.

I shook my head. "I don't think Mr. Clean knows I was looking for her. I'm sorry."

She folded her arms on the table and rested her head on them. "That's all right. I know my daughter. She won't cooperate.

We probably have a few more days before she succumbs and disappears."

Wayne started to say something, then shook his head. Good. Angela didn't know all that I'd learned online about trafficking. It was enough to curl her straight hair and steal her hope. I pushed to my feet. Holding on to what hope and bravery I had left, I went upstairs to change.

After dressing in the same clothes I'd worn at the warehouse, I rejoined the others downstairs. Somehow, I didn't think a jogging outfit, no matter how pretty it had once been, would fit in where I was going.

Wayne had changed from jeans and a tee shirt to a tailored business suit. Wowsa! If I weren't so crazy in love with Matt, and Wayne wasn't dating my sister, I might consider asking him out. "You clean up good. But, why so fancy?"

"I'm a business man just off work and out for a little sordid fun." He marched outside and to my Mercedes.

I guessed he was taking the charade all the way. I hugged Sadie, Mary Ann, and Angela, took a deep breath. "Promise you'll take the dog and cats if I don't come back."

"You'll come back," Mary Ann said, squeezing my hands. "But, I promise."

I followed Wayne, praying it wasn't the last time I'd see what was left of my family. I clicked my seatbelt into place and closed my eyes to pray for safety. For me, for Wayne, for Matt, for Cherokee, for those left at the house. The list seemed never-ending, going in a ceaseless circle like a ring on a finger.

"Are you okay?" Wayne asked.

I opened my eyes. "I will be, once this is over."

"It'll be over soon." He turned his attention back to the road. "We'll get your niece and Matt back with no more than a few scars to give them fuel for future stories."

If only it were that simple. I feared my niece might be scarred beyond repair. Instead of voicing my fear, I nodded and stared out the window as Wayne pulled the car to the shoulder of the road in front of our destination.

The Pink Flamingo, a U-shaped atrocity once painted the color of a pink flamingo, now looked as if it had a bad case of leprosy. Gray stucco showed through faded paint. The neon sign, in the shape of a giant flamingo, of course, stated the place was closed.

"There are no cars." I glanced at Wayne. "Maybe Brian is wrong."

"Don't jump to conclusions."

A truck, wearing a sign that stated Worth's Auto Shop, peeled rubber from a side road. "Brian and Miranda both mentioned the old man at the auto shop," I said. "Follow that truck."

Wayne yanked the wheel and stepped on the gas sending us speeding after Worth. The man slowed near an intersection and turned right. We followed him into the parking lot.

"Stay in the car with your head down," Wayne said, sliding from the car. "Crack your window if you want to hear, but pretend to be cowed." He straightened his tie and followed Worth as the man exited his truck.

"I'm closed today," Worth said.

"I just want you to take a look. I, uh, need to take her back to…well, she needs to be somewhere and the car is stuttering." Wayne motioned his head toward the car.

I peeked at them through the safety of my hair. When Worth glanced over, I turned away, playing the part to the best of my ability.

"They let you take her away for a while?" Worth's voice radiated with anger. "They won't even let me pay! They don't do credit, they said." He cursed. "I guess only a rich man like yourself can sample the goods. Fix your own car." He started to turn away.

Wayne grabbed his arm and yanked him back, bending close to the little man's face. "Consider yourself lucky. If you had bought one of those girls, I'd have to beat you within an inch of your life." He patted the man down, then shoved him toward the building. "Let's go."

"Who are you? Where are you taking me?"

"I'm just going to make sure you can't cause any problems for a few hours." Wayne shoved him again.

I couldn't help but grin to know that at least one scumbag was being put in his place.

It took Wayne fifteen minutes to return. By then, the sun was setting over the trees. It would be a lot harder to see when it was dark. Country roads were not known for their abundance of street lights. Not to mention the bad things that came out at night.

"The little bugger was tougher than he looked," Wayne said, sliding behind the steering wheel. "It took two hits to the head to knock him unconscious."

"I would say police brutality, but I won't."

"Good. Because it wouldn't have stopped me." He turned us back toward the motel. "He'll manage to get free of the tie I used to bind his hands once he wakes up, so we probably only have an hour before he wakes up. Then, a bit more time for him to get out of the room I locked him in. Maybe two hours, tops."

"This is rather…unorthodox, isn't it? I mean, I don't think even Matt would take me along on something of this magnitude no matter how much I fought to go." I scooted closer to the door.

He cut me a sideways glance. "I'm not Matt."

"You are a police officer, though. That means you could be in serious trouble taking along a civilian."

"You don't trust me?" A shadow passed over his eyes. "It wasn't me shooting at you this morning."

"Maybe you let me come along so you could turn me over to Bomberg and his boss." I gripped the door handle, prepared to bolt at the slightest hint I might be onto something.

"Now, you're being paranoid." He turned the car rather sharply down a road that led to the back of the motel.

"Mom said it was someone close to us. Who, other than Matt, is close to this family?"

"I'm not the bad guy, Stormi." He pulled into a pothole-filled parking lot, sporting several expensive cars. "Bingo." He pulled out his cell phone. "I'm calling for backup now. Believe what you want. I'm putting a stop to this now."

I half listened as he gave our location. It seemed as if the person on the other end was law enforcement, but I was following Mom's advice and not trusting anyone.

Someone darted around the corner of the motel and ducked behind a metal trash bin. They peeked over the edge. Heather!

I cut a glance at Wayne, grabbed my backpack, and thrust open the door. "Do what you gotta do," I told him. "I'm talking to that girl."

Somehow, someway, I was going to get Heather to tell me where Cherokee and Matt were.

20

Wayne hissed my name, then cursed, and called me a bunch of other girl names in a failed attempt to remember my alias. I ignored him and continued my mad race after Heather, losing my shoes in the process.

"Please, stop." I leaned against the side of the motel and put a hand over my heart. The poor muscle was seriously overworked and striving to pump blood through my body at a normal rate.

Heather stopped, hung her head for a second, then turned. "You must really want to die."

"Not really, but I promised Dakota I would help you. Not to mention that I'm trying to get my niece and boyfriend back." I straightened. "Do you know where they are?"

An aluminum can rattled in the parking lot behind us. I grabbed Heather and yanked her behind a steel dumpster, my other hand already reaching into my backpack for my gun.

Her eyes widened when she saw the Glock. "Maybe you won't die after all."

"I'm not planning on either one of us meeting God today." I peered over the top of the dumpster. I didn't see anyone, not even Wayne. So much for him being worried about me.

"Let's go." I stood and took Heather's hand. "Which way?"

"Your niece is in a back room of the manager's office." She pointed. "Your boyfriend is being held somewhere else." She scrunched up her face. "We were there, not too long ago. Yes," she grinned. "he's in a warehouse not far from where the party was."

"Some party," I muttered. My heart sank. We'd been so close to finding him. "Cherokee first, then Matt. Show me."

"Show you what?"

I swear I died for a second. I whirled and punched Wayne in the chest. "Are you crazy? I have a gun!"

"Why did you run off?" He crossed his arms. "You need me in case you run into one of those guys."

"He has a point," Heather said, shrinking against me. "He's very big."

I studied him for a few seconds. There really wasn't much of a choice. Trust him and pray I wasn't a fool, or try and go it alone. I chose to trust. "Cherokee is behind the manager's office. Matt is in a warehouse."

"We get your niece, let the authorities handle the bad guys, and we go get Matt." Wayne gave a definitive nod. "Follow me, and no more running off on your own. I can't split myself in two to guard you and rescue Angela's child."

"Ah." My heart warmed toward him. Sometimes I really was dense. It all made sense now. "You're breaking the rules because you love my sister."

"Yeah. Even with all her faults, I adore her. Let's go make her happy."

"Agreed." I prayed I could get my love back, too.

With my hand on Wayne's back and

Heather glued to my side, the three of us dashed toward the building. Clouds skittered across the sky, blocking the moon's light and providing us with the cover of darkness.

"This way." Heather tugged my arm. "There's a back way in. That's how I got out."

Wait. I stopped. "If you know about the back way, then your abductors do." I narrowed my eyes. "You wanted us to catch you."

Her eyes shimmered with tears. "They made me. Please. They said if I brought you to them, they'd let me go."

"They're lying." I spit out the words, angered and frustrated. "They can't let you go. Wayne?"

It was too late. Three men stepped around the corner of the building. One grabbed Heather and shoved her inside a back door. The other two held guns on Wayne and me while the first guy removed our weapons and took my backpack.

"This way." He motioned for us to enter through the door Heather had gone through. "Turn right."

A door ahead of us had a plaque with the words Manager's Office stenciled in black on a shiny brass finish. I risked a glance at Wayne. Maybe we'd get to Cherokee after all. The problem would be getting back out.

One of our escorts rapped his knuckles on the door. A voice commanded us to enter.

We stepped into a room decorated as nice as any CEO corporate office. Behind a polished cherry wood desk sat Mom's boyfriend, Robert Smithfield. This is who I wasn't supposed to trust.

I launched myself in his direction, sliding across the slippery desk and into his lap. His office chair toppled, taking us both to the floor. My hands grappled for his neck. "You shot my mother!"

"Get her off me!" He rolled out from under me, aiming a kick that took me high on the leg.

I screamed and scrambled after him again, until one of the men grabbed me around the waist and heaved me off of Robert as if I weighed nothing more than a child. "You'll pay for this."

"Hurting your mother is one of my greatest regrets," Robert said, righting his chair. He motioned for them to release me. "Please, have a seat."

"No." I wouldn't do anything he requested.

One of the men punched Wayne in the stomach, doubling him over.

"Fine." I plopped in a burgundy vinyl chair that whooshed under me. "Now what?"

"It's a real pity you aren't ten years younger," he said. "But, I have a buyer who will pay top dollar for you, Stormi Nelson."

"Excuse me?" Someone wanted me? "Why?"

"You're famous."

"A lot of people are famous."

"He likes the way you look." Robert shrugged. "You're a beautiful woman, still relatively young and of breeding age, not to mention the fact your mother said you were a virgin. I don't turn down a fair offer."

I couldn't help but ask, "How much?"

"Fifty thousand dollars."

That left me speechless. I had no idea I was worth that much. "I won't allow you to sell me."

"We have ways of breaking you." He grinned and rubbed his chin. "I do admit that your niece is tough to crack. Solitary confinement doesn't do the trick with her as it does with most girls. Perhaps, it won't work with you, either."

I did like my solitude, but wasn't about to tell him that. "I want to see her."

"Oh, you will. In fact, you'll be right next to her." He motioned toward one of his goons, who yanked me to my feet and pulled me past a very subdued Wayne, who stood with a gun to his head.

"Take him, too," Robert said. "Put him with his partner. The two of them will fetch a good price for slave labor."

Wayne snorted. "As if we'll allow that."

"Then, we'll kill you. I'm finished talking. Have a good day." He leaned back in his chair and propped his feet on his desk.

I yanked free and ran toward him

again, hands reaching for his throat. I didn't make it two steps before someone hit me in the back of the head and I crumpled to the floor.

When I woke, I was handcuffed to a metal cot. Across the room, on another cot, was Cherokee, wearing the skimpiest American Indian costume I'd ever seen. Other than that, she looked wonderful and unharmed.

She blinked at me like an owl trying to focus. "Aunt Stormi? Why is your hair black?"

"Oh, thank God. It's a disguise." I sat up. "Are you okay? They haven't hurt you, have they?"

"No. They keep waiting for me to be a bit nicer, is how they put it." She grinned and swung her legs over the cot. "Other than being bored, locking me in here isn't going to get me to do anything I don't want to do. They threatened to drug me, but I told them I'd kill myself and they'd be wanted for murder. As stupid as that sounds, they left me alone. Robert said it was only a matter of time until this room drove me to the point I'd do anything to get out." She blinked away moisture gathering in her eyes. "I was almost there."

"Are you tied to the bed?"

She shook her head and came over to sit next to me. "I don't have anything to pick the lock with."

"That's okay. My hands are so skinny they'll slide out if they're wet. I need you to spit on them."

"Gross." She frowned.

"It's not gross for you. Do you want out of here or not?" My writing research was bound to come in handy sooner or later. And, since I was blessed with being able to almost curl my hands in half sideways, my idea might just work.

"I don't have enough spit," Cherokee said. "They barely give me food and water."

"Then lick around the cuffs. I need my hands to be as wet as possible." I swallowed against the nausea as she licked my hands. The wet, rough texture threatened to gag me. When I thought she'd wet them enough, I twisted and turned, ignoring the steel biting into my skin.

"You're starting to bleed." Cherokee stared into my face. "Shouldn't you stop?"

"Not if we want out of here." I groaned and gave a big yank. My hands pulled free. I stared at the cuts and ripped skin around my wrists. "They'll heal."

Pushing past the pain, I went to the door and peered out the tiny window. I didn't see a guard, so tried the door handle. I glanced at Cherokee.

"I guess they figured you wouldn't get loose. They told me if I left, they'd kill Mom. Where is she? Why didn't she come with you?"

"Seriously? You wanted me to bring the drama queen?"

"You're right. Mom would have gone into hysterics after one look at me."

"Yep. That outfit would have sent her over the edge." I couldn't help but wonder what Robert would have dressed me in. A sexy author? I'd have to wonder later. "Let's go. Quick and quiet."

I stepped into the hall and looked both ways. We hadn't been held in a regular motel room. Maybe a former supply closet? Stretching in front of us were numbered doors. One of the doors started to open. I shoved Cherokee back into the closet. Business proceeded as usual.

"How long was I unconscious?"

"Maybe a half hour."

It could be an hour or more before authorities arrived, according to Wayne's calculations. I assumed help would come from Little Rock. An hour was too long. I had to get to Matt. Now that Robert also had Wayne, I didn't believe for a minute that he planned on selling them to the highest bidder. Not two headstrong men, no matter how big and strong they were. My instincts told me they'd be dead before the sun came up.

I checked the hall again. Empty. I darted out, Cherokee close behind, and headed right. The hall seemed shorter in that direction. If we could get to the parking lot, and find an older model vehicle, I could hotwire it. Another time when my research would come in handy.

We pushed through a door that led to the pool, or what was left of it. No water filled the cracking tiled hole. On our far right was a gate. Beyond that, were a few parked vehicles. I grabbed Cherokee's hand and raced for freedom.

The gate was locked. I bent over and cupped my hands. "I'll give you a boost."

"What about you?"

"I'll…" I glanced around and spotted a large terra cotta planter. "Help me move this."

We shoved against it until it moved, filling the quiet night with the screech of plaster against cement. I cringed and shoved harder.

"Okay, up and over. Be careful landing on the other side."

Cherokee climbed over like the nimble girl she was. Me, I took a bit longer. My arms threatened not to hold me long enough for me to get a leg over.

"Hey!" A deep voice shouted.

I found the strength I needed and hurtled after my niece.

21

"The van!" I yanked open the door to an early model panel van and locked the doors. Bingo! These people weren't the brightest marble in the bag. The keys dangled from the ignition. I had the van started before Cherokee's door slammed shut.

With one terrified glance at the armed man sprinting toward us, I pressed the gas pedal and squealed tires racing to the road. "They'll figure out where we're headed soon enough," I said. "I'm dropping you off at the safest place I can find."

"I'm going with you."

"No, you're not." That was the last thing I wanted. She'd been through enough.

"Please. I can create a distraction.

Matt was beat up because of me."

I cut her a sideways glance, then whipped my attention back to the road as we careened around a corner. "Explain."

"They were trying to drug me. He gave up his cover to stop them. I have to help." She crossed her arms over her skimpy top. "Besides, I'm legally an adult. You can't stop me."

True. But, my heart still ached to think of her remaining in danger for another second.

"All I know about where Matt might be is a warehouse close to the party. Any ideas?" I accelerated once we reached a straight stretch of road.

"There is a smaller one that I saw men coming in and out of before they put me in the cell at the party. It has a dark green door."

Not the easiest thing to see in the dark. "Search the van for a weapon of some sort. They took my gun." Robert, the snake. It was good for him that they took my gun. Mom would be heartbroken when she woke up. She might have had her suspicions toward the end, but she had really seemed to like him. *Please, God, let her wake up.*

"Oh. My. Gosh!" Cherokee dropped a small gun into my lap. "That's a nine-millimeter, I think." She sat a small camera-type bag on her seat. "There's ammo in there. We can do this, Aunt Stormi. I found a flashlight and another gun." She climbed back into her seat, wearing a black windbreaker.

"Put the other gun in the bag."

"No way. I know how to shoot. You don't want to know who taught me." She took a shuddering breath. "Remember that boyfriend I told you about? The one I really liked?"

"I don't remember his name."

"It doesn't matter." She sniffed. "We went on a date one night. Then, instead of taking me home, he took me to Robert's house."

I sensed there was more to the story. More that would increase my desire to see Robert at the end of my gun, but I didn't press. I'd find her the best counselor money could buy when this was all behind us. "Not all men are scum. Just remember that."

"I will. I'm going to find someone like Matt." She gave a sad smile. "If he wasn't with you, I'd try to steal him."

I laughed. "He's too old for you."

"There!" She pointed to a poorly paved road off the side of the highway. "I remember this road."

I yanked the wheel to the right, almost taking out the van's front end with a pot hole. The moment the back of a metal building came into sight, I turned off the headlights and slowed our speed.

Three buildings, all identical from the back, formed a half circle around a parking lot resembling a cement version of Swiss cheese. Rather than bounce our way across, I parked. "Stay close. I gripped the gun and opened the van door.

So far, it didn't seem as if our abductors knew we'd come to rescue Matt. They most likely thought I'd taken Cherokee as far away as possible. Something I wish I could have done, but couldn't risk. Not when Matt's life hung in the balance.

"This way." I tapped Cherokee's

shoulder and motioned for her to follow me between two buildings. What a story I'd have to write about. Here I was, me…Stormi Nelson…scaredy-cat extraordinaire, on a mission to rescue the man I love and free some young women from slavery. I thanked God I had the bravery when I needed it, because once this was all over, I doubted I'd have an ounce left.

"The green door." Cherokee pointed.

With my heart in my throat, I slithered along the perimeter of the building, gun at the ready, and pulled on every resource of research I'd ever done on writing suspenseful adventure stories. If I focused on that, maybe my heart wouldn't pound with such ferocity my chest moved with every beat.

Cherokee's normal olive complexion appeared unearthly pale in the moonlight. I must look like a wraith. I grasped her hand and squeezed. "Ready?"

She nodded.

I pushed open the door, wincing at its metallic screech. When I heard no further noise, I stepped inside a hall so dark, I could barely see my hand in front of my face.

Cherokee clicked on the flashlight, illuminating a cavernous room, and handed me the light. At the far end was a desk, several large plastic crates, and a door. I prayed with all I had in me that Matt was on the other side of that door.

The sound of a car engine outside spurred us across the room like horses in a race. I slid to a halt at the door and peered through a window placed at eye level. I shined the light inside. Matt sat against a wall, his arms wrapped around his knees. I rapped on the glass.

He glanced up. I almost fell to my knees at the sight of his swollen eyes and split lip. I blinked away tears and tried the doorknob. "Look in that desk for a key."

The sounds of things being moved around still didn't pull me away from the sight of my beloved. I wouldn't break eye contact until I had to.

"Someone's coming." Cherokee thrust a key ring in my hand and took the flashlight. "Hurry. They turned off their car." She grabbed a broom from next to the desk and ducked behind a crate.

Good girl. Ears peeled for the sound of the main door opening, I tried key after key. The fifth one slipped into the lock with a click. I flung the door open and rushed to Matt's side. "Can you walk?"

He nodded and pushed to his feet, groaning with the effort.

I thrust my shoulder under his arm. "Have you seen Wayne? They took him over an hour ago."

"I heard…them put someone…in a crate."

Oh, God. In a crate, like an animal.

We exited the room and scurried behind the same crate as Cherokee, who was peering through an eye-sized hole. "He's in here."

The warehouse door opened. The three of us froze. Other than where we crouched, there was nowhere to hide. I held my gun tighter as Cherokee clicked off her light. Harsh overhead fluorescents flickered to life.

Matt's arm around me tightened. "Give me the gun."

I shook my head. Cherokee was much

more obedient and handed him the small case she'd hung around her neck. "In there."

He slipped his arm free of me and opened the case, checked to make sure the gun was loaded, it was, and stepped in front of us. From his hunched-over posture, every move had to be agony. Still, rather than let me take care of him, he still wanted to protect us. God must have broken the mold after making my man.

"I cannot believe you let her get away." Robert's voice echoed. "Find her and the girl and find them now!"

"Uh, boss, the cop is gone."

Expletives exploded so loud and harsh, I almost covered my ears. "The other one isn't loose. I can see the lock from here."

"Come on in and finish the job," Wayne taunted from inside. "I'm sure the three of you can take on one beaten man. Especially with two guns."

Three of them, three of us. We had two guns and a broom. Still, we were fighting for our lives, which was still a stronger motive than the almighty dollar.

"Don't do anything until I say so," Matt whispered. He cupped my cheek. "Don't be a hero."

"Ditto." I leaned into his touch, warmed by the love in his eyes. If today was our last day, it would be our last day together.

"For crying out loud, stop the mush," Wayne whispered. "They're letting me out. I want you to put an end to this. Hey! Use a lover's touch, please." His snarky comments alerted us to the fact he was no longer in the crate.

"Take him to the river and dump him," Robert said.

"I don't think so." I stepped out, gun aimed at his head.

Matt exhaled sharply and followed.

Cherokee stayed hidden. She might not have a deadly weapon, but she could still launch a surprise attack if things took a turn for the worse.

"The lovely Stormi." Robert grinned and perched on the corner of the desk. His foot swung back and forth. "A pity you colored your hair, but my buyers won't care."

I pulled the trigger, shooting him in the foot. I immediately prayed for forgiveness, mostly because the sight of him clutching his foot and writhing on the ground brought me a lot of sinful pleasure. "The gig is up, gentlemen. Hand your weapons to my sweetheart or the next bullet takes your boss in the head." Not that I could go as far as to kill him, no matter how much I detested the man. But, my show of force told them I might.

They dropped their weapons. The clatter rang through the room with a sound as pretty as a boy's choir. To add to the music was the whine of sirens pulling into the parking lot. We'd done it.

The moment ten police officers barged through the door, I lowered my hand and sagged to the floor. Matt joined me, leaning his head back and closing his eyes.

"Woman, you have guts." Wayne squatted in front of me, grinning from ear-to-ear. Blood dribbled from the cut on his cheek. "I was prepared to meet my maker. I owe you my life. You and that lovely niece of yours." He held his hand out to Cherokee. "Are you okay?"

She nodded, then marched over to Robert, who was being hauled to his feet by two police officers. She stared at him for a second, then slapped him. The sound cast everyone into a stunned silence, then the room exploded into applause by every officer there.

I grinned. That's my niece.

When the paramedics arrived, I allowed them to help me to my feet. I refused to leave Matt's side, and Wayne promised to look after Cherokee. We insisted the four of us ride to the hospital together. We'd been apart long enough.

"I need to borrow a phone." I glanced at one of the paramedics.

He handed me a cell phone. I called Angela to let her know I had Cherokee and that we were headed to the hospital. I could barely hear her words over her sobbing, but I could have sworn she promised me everything under the moon.

Glancing at Matt lying on the gurney, I knew I already had everything I wanted.

Except the ability to breathe. I took in

huge gulps of air.

Matt stretched a hand out to me.

"I—" Darkness overtook me, and I fell.

22

I woke to the sound of beeping. A tiled ceiling hung over me and something heavy rested on my legs. Frantic, I thrashed, only to discover I was in a hospital bed covered with several blankets. I released a deep breath and turned my head.

"Mama?" I hadn't called her that since I was a child. Still, I jumped from the bed and rushed to her side. "You're awake."

She smiled. "It takes more than a knock on the head to put this girl down." She caressed my face. "How are you? I hear you're quite the hero."

"I'm not. God gave me a burst of what I needed, when I needed it." I entwined my fingers with hers. "Why am I here?"

"You collapsed in the ambulance is what Wayne said, and you've been out for a few hours. What a nice man. He's been catering to my every need, and making sure Cherokee has the help she needs. And, this is the most amazing part. He has patience with your sister."

I laughed and rested my cheek against her hand. "Have you heard where Matt is?"

"The next room. He had a couple of cracked ribs and broken fingers, but he'll be fine."

"I hate to leave you, but—"

"Go. I'll be here when you get back."

I stood. "I'm sorry about Robert."

"I'm glad I found out what kind of a skunk he is before I married him. Now, go."

She didn't need to tell me twice. With one last glance to make sure she really was awake and talking, I left the room. Left or right? I heard Wayne's deep laugh and turned right.

"Dude, you should have seen her." Wayne sat in a mint green vinyl chair next to Matt's bed. "She was like a warrior. Didn't even trust me."

"Until it was over. Then, she crumpled like a wadded up napkin." Matt laughed and clutched his gauze-wrapped chest. "Don't make me laugh."

"Really?" I crossed my arms. "Y'all are laughing at me? After all I did for you?"

"Sweetheart." Matt beckoned for me to come closer.

"I'll leave the two of you alone," Wayne said. "I promised Angela I'd take her to lunch."

I barely acknowledged him. Matt's face drew me like a hook. I sat in the chair Wayne had vacated and let Matt take my hand. "I think I've at least proved I can be relied on in an emergency."

"No argument there. I wouldn't be lying here, if not for you." His eyes darkened. "I'd be at the bottom of the lake."

"Don't talk like that." The thought sent an ice cold river of dread through me. I'd come too close to losing him. "I thought Oak Meadows was a peaceful town."

"All towns have their secrets."

"Let's move to the middle of nowhere." How sweet that sounded. "I can write as long as I have a computer and internet."

"Don't tempt me." He grimaced and moved to a sitting position.

I placed a pillow behind his back for added support.

"Come here." Matt patted the bed.

"I'll hurt you."

"It's worth it." He patted again.

I scrambled up beside him and nestled close, wrapping my arms around him, careful not to squeeze, although everything in me wanted to hold him tight and never let him go. "I love you, Matthew Steele. I'd storm the gates of Hades again if it meant bringing you home."

"I know now is not the right place, but, will you—"

"Stormi!" Angela burst into the room and darted to my side of the bed. "When Wayne told me you were awake, I said I had to see you before we went to eat." She yanked me from the bed and drew me to her surgery-enhanced bosom. "Words do not express my thanks for bringing my baby home."

Cherokee hung back, letting her mother gush. I waved her forward, relieved to see the color back in her cheeks and a bit of a sparkle in her eyes. What a difference a night at home makes to a young woman.

"Are you okay?" I searched her face.

"I will be. Thanks to you." She planted a kiss on my cheek. "Me and those other girls will be just fine."

I freed myself from my sister's suffocating hold and pulled my niece close. "You were a huge help in freeing Matt. I should be thanking you."

"Enough." Matt frowned. "I was getting ready to ask Stormi something. Could all of you leave?"

He had been going to ask me a question. My heart leaped. "Leave. Now." I waved my arms, ushering them out like a bunch of baby chicks. When they were out of the room, I started to climb back next to Matt.

"Good morning, Mr. Steele." A doctor entered the room and lifted Matt's chart from a hook next to the bed. "How are those ribs? The fingers?"

I groaned and plopped into the chair. A hospital had too many distractions. "When does he get to go home?"

"If he's feeling fine, I'll release him now. You, too, since you seem to be none the worse for wear after your collapse."

Angela didn't get to go to lunch. Instead, Wayne drove a van full of three hospital released patients. I sat in the back with Matt, while Mom sat in the middle with Cherokee, and Angela rode shotgun. When we pulled into the driveway, Dakota bounded from the front porch, Sadie at his side and dashed toward us. My cats, Ebony and Ivory, greeted us from the other side of the window. I was home and surrounded by family.

Wayne helped us from the van. As we made our way up the front steps, Mary Ann opened the door with a flourish. "Welcome home!"

I laughed as I stepped into the kitchen. She must have raided the freezer of what was left of my frozen casseroles. Now, I had a reason to make more. Something I did when I wanted to relax, and after the past week, nothing sounded better than relaxation. Except for me to hear the question Matt was going to ask.

We crowded around the kitchen table. It felt like Thanksgiving, which in a way, I suppose it was. I know my heart was so full of thanks to God, I thought it would burst.

Several times during our meal of assorted casseroles, my gaze connected with Matt's. He would smile, as if he held a secret, then turn to speak to someone else. Oh, but I did love watching him. The way his hair fell forward across one eye when it wasn't slicked back. The way a dimple winked from his cheek when he laughed, or how his eyes sparkled when someone said something humorous. My man was definitely the product of a Master Craftsman.

Mom's hand trailed across my shoulders on the way to the coffeepot. A lump formed in my throat. How would I have gone on without her?

"I propose a toast." Dakota held up a red plastic cup filled with soda. "To my Aunt Stormi. The greatest kick a…uh, butt person I know."

"Here, here!" The others raised their cups.

I let the tears fall. Surely, they were all used to my emotions by now.

Matt stood, the pain it caused him etched on his face. He came around the table and held out his hand. "This isn't going to happen unless I make it happen. Being alone is virtually impossible with this family."

I smiled through my tears. "Yes!"

"I haven't asked yet." He laughed and slowly got to one knee. "Stormi Nelson, best-selling author and heroine in her own right, will you marry me and make me the happiest man God ever created?"

"Can I say yes now?" I tugged on his hand so he would stand.

He nodded.

"Yes." I wrapped my arms around his neck and kissed him with all the love in my heart while my family cheered around us.

~

Stay tuned for the next misadventure of Stormi, *Poison Bubbles*, where planning a wedding is more than merely stressful. It's deadly.

Enjoy other mysteries by Cynthia Hickey

Nosy Neighbor Series
Anything For A Mystery, Book 1
A Killer Plot, Book 2
Skin Care Can Be Murder, Book 3

The Summer Meadows Series
Fudge-Laced Felonies, Book 1
Candy-Coated Secrets, Book 2
Chocolate-Covered Crime, Book 3
Maui Macadamia Madness, Book 4
All four novels in one collection

The River Valley Mystery Series
Deadly Neighbors, Book 1
Advance Notice, Book 2
The Librarian's Last Chapter, Book 3
All three novels in one collection

See Cynthia's other books at
www.cynthiahickey.com

ABOUT THE AUTHOR

Website at www.cynthiahickey.com

Multi-published and Amazon and ECPA Best-Selling author Cynthia Hickey has sold close to a million copies of her works since 2013. She has taught a Continuing Education class at the 2015 American Christian Fiction Writers conference, several small ACFW chapters and RWA chapters, and small writer retreats. She and her husband run the small press, Winged Publications, which includes some of the CBA's best well-known authors. She lives in Arizona and Arkansas, becoming a snowbird, with her husband and one dog. She has ten grandchildren who keep her busy and tell everyone they know that "Nana is a writer".

Connect with me on FaceBook

Twitter

Bookbub

Sign up for my newsletter and receive
a free short story
www.cynthiahickey.com

Follow me on Amazon

www.ingramcontent.com/pod-product-compliance
Lightning Source LLC
Chambersburg PA
CBHW061025120726
47910CB00006B/2105